GUARDIANS OF THE SAGE

GUARDIANS OF THE SAGE

HARRY SINCLAIR DRAGO

M. EVANS
Essex, Connecticut

Published by M. Evans
An imprint of The Globe Pequot Publishing Group, Inc.
64 South Main Street
Essex, CT 06426
www.globepequot.com

British Library Cataloguing in Publication Information Available

Library of Congress Cataloging-in-Publication Data

Library of Congress Control Number: 2014947819

ISBN: 978-1-59077-474-8 (pbk.)
ISBN: 978-1-59077-475-5 (electronic)

Bob, you used to work for old Slick-ear—only you had another name for him. Today you go to town in an automobile. You've traded the jingling of spur chains for the rattling of a Ford truck. You speak learnedly of tractors and Diesel engines.

Well, it was not always so. You knew that big sweep of country between Quinn River and the Steen Mountains when it *was* country and a pair of chaps didn't make a man a top-hand.

Maybe I've scrambled my geography a little—maybe I've taken some liberties with the names of men and places; but you'll be able to correct that and to understand why it was necessary.

It is September. The aspens in the little parks above the ranger's cabin must be all gold and yellow now. Old National and Buckskin will be looming up as though they were only a stone's throw away. The deer will be moving toward the rimrocks. The memory is still sharp with me.

I'd like to be back there with you and young Hank. I want to see the high places again, Bob; I want to smell the sage.

CONTENTS

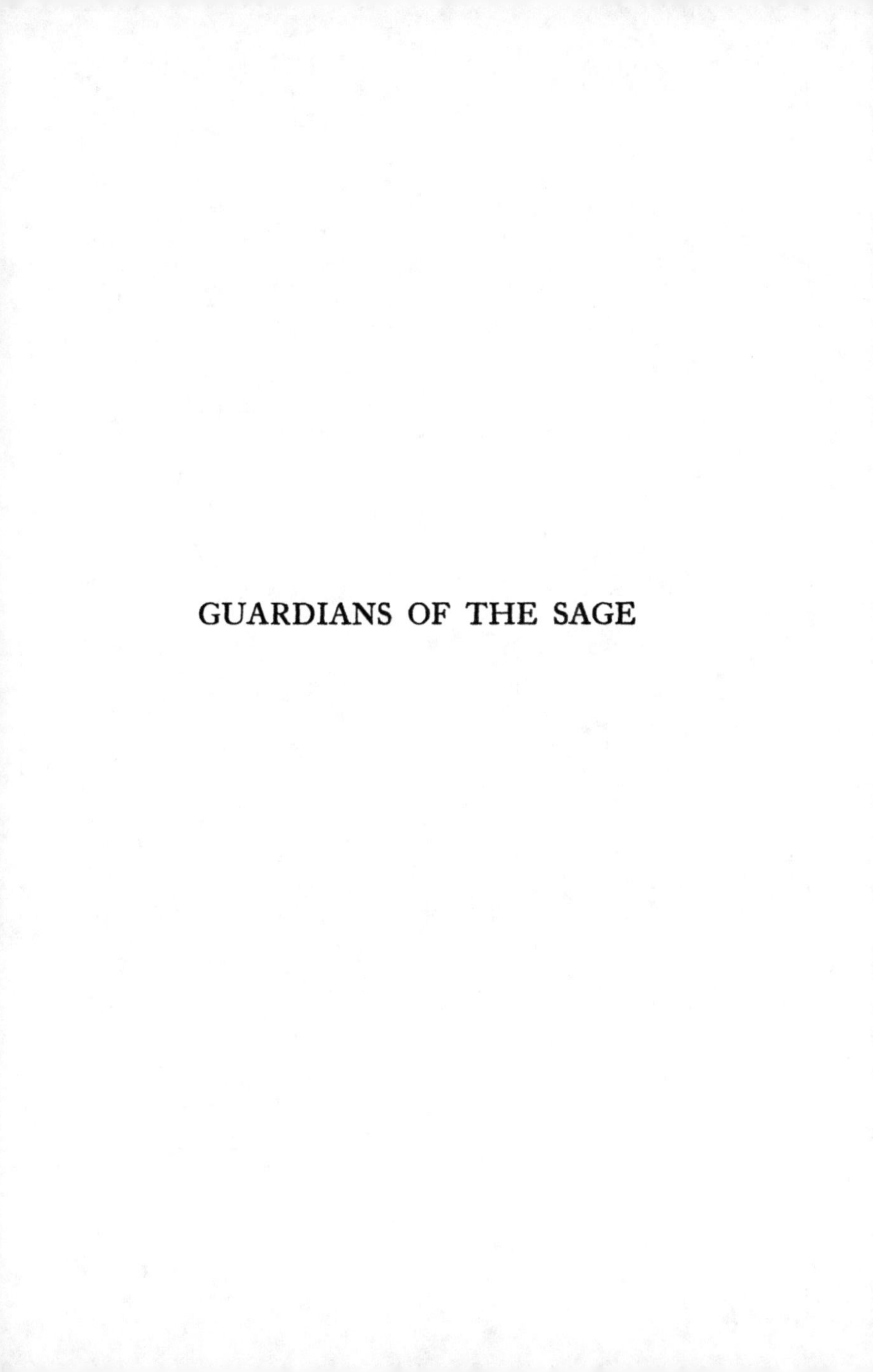

GUARDIANS OF THE SAGE

CHAPTER I

RANGE HOG

THE long twilight of late June was fading rapidly into night as a horseman crested the low hills to the east of the Willow Vista Ranch. Momentarily, man and beast were silhouetted against the skyline, for behind them the moon was already tipping the mountain-desert with silver.

Both bore evidence of a slashing ride.

A tight-lipped grunt of satisfaction escaped the man as he caught his first glimpse of the distant lights that marked the ranch-house—pale, buttery daubs of yellow, glowing dimly against the black bulk of the Steen Mountains beyond.

"Old Slick-ear better be there," he grumbled desperately as he raked his horse with his spurs.

The big dun, obviously winded, was heaving violently, its distended nostrils blood-flecked. The spurs bit cruelly. The horse trembled and tried to hold back, eyes rolling wildly. Heart and lungs were bursting, and fear—not unlike that known to humans—was clamping its icy fingers on the animal.

The man realized that the end was not far away. By choice, he was not a killer of horses; but the business on which he rode was urgent enough to make him reckless of horseflesh as well as himself. The news he brought was important, and in the end, minutes would spell the difference between success and failure.

The way was down hill now, a scant two miles.

The horse plunged onward in a last gallant effort. The man's eyes were alert, as though expecting the animal to go down any moment. Danger to himself was great, unless he managed to jump clear. He was not unmindful of it, nor was he unmoved by the dun's gameness. Since late afternoon, they had covered the fifty long, desert miles that lay between the Bar S on the South Fork of the Owyhee and the home ranch on Rebel Creek.

The man had come even farther. He had been in the saddle since morning. The horse he rode now was the fourth that had served him that day. He was not an emotional man, but the dun happened to belong to him. Maybe that made a difference.

"I reckon if there's a horse heaven you'll just about reach it, Baldy," he muttered grimly, a tortured look in his eyes. But of course a man gets to know a horse rather well in four years.

Suddenly the wooden bridge at Rebel Creek loomed out of the darkness at him. A tattoo of flying hoofs rang out sharp and pregnant with alarm as the dun thundered across the planks. In the stillness of the early evening the drumming echoed and re-echoed across the valley until it reached the house.

Supper was over, but two men and a girl sat at the long table in the dining-room, memorandum books and a pile of freight bills spread out before them. All three looked up sharply.

"What was that?" the girl asked apprehensively. Her father, seated across the table, was busy with his note-books again. He smiled to himself over her anxiety.

"Just somebody crossing the bridge, Letty," he said.

"Whoever it is, he ain't losin' no time," the other man remarked. He was Joe Tracey, the foreman of Willow Vista. "He's sure comin' fast," he added to himself. His thin face was hawk-like in the lamplight.

Letty Stall went to the open window and peered out, but she could not see anything. The moon was just beginning to peep over the hills to the east. Even as she tarried at the window, it grew lighter. Presently, she could make out a moving smudge of blackness in the dark. Recognition was still impossible.

Just why a madly driven horse at this hour of the evening should tighten her throat with a premonition of trouble, she could not say. Usually it meant sickness or possibly the death of one of her father's men— something that had been happening ever since Old Henry had brought her up from San Francisco to spend her first summer on one of the Bar S ranches.

But that was years ago. She was twenty now, and if San Francisco regarded her only as a charming debutante, she was quite used to the exigencies of ranch life, with doctors and hospitals miles away. Still, it in no way explained the feeling that gripped her to-night.

Eastern Oregon was a new country. Stall and Matlack had done well in Harney and Malheur counties. They owned no less than eleven ranches in that big sweep of country between the Steen Mountains and the Snake, an empire unto themselves. Their brand, the Bar S, was as well-known—and hated—there as it long had been in Nevada and certain parts of California.

Steve Matlack was no longer active in the affairs of Bar S. In the truest sense, he never had been active. From the beginning, Henry Stall had been the moving force behind their success. He had led the invasion into Nevada, and later into Oregon.

He had been in the Steen Mountain country for twelve years now—a period in which he had never failed to arrogate to himself all the rights and privileges of a reigning monarch. What he wanted, he took; and he managed to keep it, too—either with the aid of the courts or without them. It was his boast that he had never vented a brand of his on horse or steer, nor sold an acre of land once he had acquired it.

Letty knew the feeling against her father often ran high. Cowmen called him a range hog. Threats had been made against his life. Only a few days back, over in Harney Valley, he had been fired on from ambush. If the bullet had missed him it was because the shot had been intended only as a warning.

It had not deterred him. She knew nothing could

change her father. He would go on grabbing land and water rights, running more and more cattle, until he died. Trouble was sure to come of it, sooner perhaps than he supposed, and as she stood at the window, her blood thinning, she could not throw off the depressing feeling that, whoever the rider was, his business there brought that day nearer.

The moon hung low above the hills now, bathing the valley with its soft glow. Barns and corrals gleamed whitely. The oncoming horse splashed across the shallow irrigation ditch that supplied the ranch truck-patch, lashing the water to spray. As it fell back, the moonlight touched it and it glistened like tiny particles of silver tinsel drifting on the air.

"Who is it?" old Henry asked.

"Can't make out," Tracey answered, his eyes screwed into a piercing squint. Across the yard, someone came to the door of the bunkhouse and held up a lighted lantern. "We'll know in a minute who it is."

The old man leaned over the table and peered out with the others, his face, ruddy against the gray of his closely-cropped hair, as stolid as usual.

It was only a moment or two before the horse galloped into the ranch-yard. Then, before anyone could speak, the animal crashed to earth, throwing its rider headlong.

"Rode him till he dropped!" Tracey exclaimed. "Whoever he is he got a good shakin' up." He put a leg through the window to hurry to the stranger's aid.

Men were running from the bunkhouse, too. The man who had been thrown had not moved.

"He's dead!" Letty gasped, unable to look away.

"No danger of that," her father said sourly. "It's the horse that's dead. They're cheap enough, but it's a waste of good money to ride them until they drop."

Before Tracey could climb through the window, the man sat up. He shook his head as though to clear it and then got to his feet. He was tall, and thin, almost to emaciation.

Old Henry bit at the ends of his stubby mustache. "Hunh," he muttered with genuine surprise. "That's Mr. Case of the South Fork ranch, isn't it?"

He always addressed his foreman as Mister. It was equivalent to knighthood with Bar S men.

"It's Judd as sure as shooting!" Tracey exclaimed. He turned to the old man, and his eyes were suddenly grave. "What's he doin' way over here?"

The owner of the Bar S dropped his ever-handy note-books into his pocket. Judd Case had been working for him for years. The man was altogether too level-headed to have ridden fifty miles over nothing at all.

"I daresay it won't be anything pleasant," he muttered glumly. "Good news doesn't travel fast like that."

From the conversation without, they knew Judd was not seriously hurt. The Willow Vista men started back to their quarters. A moment later, the foreman of the South Fork ranch limped into the dining-room.

Old Slick-ear looked him over as though he hoped

to discover the reason for his presence there even before Case could speak. Failing in that, he put his question into words. "What is it, Mr. Case?" he asked abruptly.

"Certainly glad to find ya here," Case replied. "Mind if I sit down? Got shook up a little." Now that he had arrived he seemed strangely unexcited. He nodded to Tracey. "Hi, Joe? And you, Miss Letty?" Unhurried, he turned to Stall once more. "I was afraid you and Miss Letty might have gone back to the Quinn River ranch, on your way south." He paused momentarily, hunting for words. "I came a right smart ways to-day, Mr. Stall. I was in Wild Horse this morning."

"Wild Horse?" the old man grunted incredulously. The others did not try to conceal their surprise. Wild Horse was a shipping point on the Oregon Short Line, and well across into Idaho. Ordinarily, it was considered a hard two-day trip.

But most of the Bar S beef was driven south to the Southern Pacific at Winnemucca. So, although Wild Horse was a county seat, being in Idaho, Stall and Matlack had little or no business there. That little was confined to the Government Land Office where the deputy commissioner for the Oywhee-Malheur district held forth.

"My blacksmith quit last week," Judd explained. "I went over to Wild Horse to see if I couldn't hire a new man. I got that attended to last night. I was waitin' around the hotel for breakfast this morning when I run into Clay Quantrell. I guess you know him. He's been freightin' out of Wild Horse and doin' a little ranchin' on the side for two or three years."

"Yes, I know him," the old man muttered, and his tone said the memory was not a pleasant one. "What about him?"

"He wanted to know if I'd been over to the land office. Well, I didn't like the way he said it," Judd went on. "I always figured he was on the other side of the fence where we were concerned. So I waited around until eight o'clock and went up to the commissioner's office. I sure got the news."

"Come, come, Mr. Case, let's have it!" old Henry exploded, impatiently. He had been making his own deductions the past few moments. "Has it anything to do with Squaw Valley?"

"You guessed it, Mr. Stall! The Government is movin' the Piutes over to Fort Hall next month. The Squaw Valley Reservation is going to be thrown open for sale."

"Well, well, no fault to find with that!" Letty saw her father rub his hands together like a money-lender. "Finest blue joint grass in Oregon!" he exclaimed. "You know I've had my heart set on it for a long while. This is the best news I've heard in months!" He actually beamed at his men as he pushed back his chair and got to his feet. "Jim Montana is still the deputy commissioner, eh?"

"Yeah," Judd answered tonelessly.

"When is he going to hold his sale?"

"To-morrow noon on the steps of the court-house in Wild Horse!"

"What . . . To-morrow moon?"

In the silence that followed, the ticking of the clock on the wall sounded loud and oppressive. Letty closed the window. Her father's face was purple with rage.

"Well, I do be damned!" Joe Tracey whipped out as he brought his chair down on all fours with a bang. It so perfectly expressed old Slick-ear's feelings that he offered no reproof, though, as a rule, he objected to profanity. "You sure you got this straight, Judd?"

"Sure I got it straight, Joe. The sale is going to be held to-morrow."

"But Montana promised to keep me informed," old Henry stormed. "He was to let me know if anything like this came up."

"Well, maybe this is his way of lettin' you know, Mr. Stall," Judd declared pointedly. "There's no use beatin' about the bush. I know Jim Montana used to work for you here. Don't let that fool you. He don't want the Bar S in Squaw Valley. If he can fix it so that the Crocketts and the Gaults and those other outfits above the reservation can grab that range and split it up between them, he's goin' to do it."

"But he can't sell an acre of that land without advertising it! The law compels him to do that!"

Judd shook his head wearily. "It's been advertised

—and mighty good care has been taken that only the right people saw it."

Letty's head went up stiffly and her brown eyes glowed with indignation as she faced the foreman of the South Fork.

"Mr Case—you're not accusing Jim Montana of anything underhanded, are you?"

Her father answered for Judd. "Underhanded?" he echoed. "What else can you call it? I've had my eyes on that reservation for ten years, because I can claim water rights in that valley! I always figured some day I'd get it. With my water and that land I'd have a cowman's paradise. Montana knew how anxious I was about it."

"Maybe he had a reason for changing his mind," Letty argued.

"What? Are you taking sides against me?" Old Henry's white mustache fairly bristled.

"Of course not, Father." She did not flinch as she had often seen men do who had thought to cross him.

"Well, you're making excuses for him. What reason do you think he had for changing his mind?"

"Maybe he feels as others do—that you've got range enough in this country. Just being opposed to you doesn't necessarily mean that he's been underhanded about anything. When he worked for you he proved himself a good man. You said so yourself."

"Pah!" he stormed. "You heard what Mr. Case

said, didn't you? I know when I've been tricked. You need not try to defend the man."

"I'm not," Letty insisted. "But there's trouble enough here now—and more coming, if I know anything about it. If Jim Montana is trying to keep you out of Squaw Valley it's only because he thinks it's the best thing for all concerned."

The head of the Bar S had to laugh, and he was not given to mirth as a rule.

"Best for himself, you mean," he said. "Well, he's had his trouble for nothing." His manner was serious enough. "I've always had to fight for what I got, and I'm going to fight now." He turned to Joe Tracey. "You have my grays hitched, Mr. Tracey. I'll be ready by the time you drive up."

Letty stared at him with fresh concern. "Father, what are you going to do?"

"I'm going to Wild Horse! I'll be there by noon to-morrow!"

"Oh, no," Letty pleaded. "Father, you're too old to make a hard trip like that——"

"Old?" he thundered. "Hunh! I'm not so old that I'll let Montana put anything over like this on me. Just hurry along, Mr. Tracey."

Judd started to follow Joe. Old Henry called him back.

"You better get your saddle and bridle, Mr. Case. You can throw them in my rig and ride back with me. That'll save sending a man back with a horse later on."

Old Slick-ear always knew how to save a day's wages. But he paid the top price, and he expected his men to earn it. His preparations for the long trip were simple. His field equipment in traveling over his ranches consisted of a nightshirt, a toothbrush and his note-books. When he returned to the dining-room, he found Letty waiting for him. Her hat lay on the table beside her.

"Father, you know you can't drive to Wild Horse by noon to-morrow."

"I don't intend to drive all the way. I'll use the grays as far as the South Fork. I'll get a fresh team there and go on to Mud Springs. I ought to make the Springs by daylight. I'll get a saddle horse from Ed Ducker and go into Wild Horse with time to spare." Letty was drawing on her gloves. The old man's eyes clouded as he watched her. "Where are you going?"

"With you," she answered without hesitation.

"Hunh?" he grunted, his jaws working nervously. "Say, look here, Letty, this isn't any lark: I don't mind your defying me around here; but I'm not taking you into Wild Horse. It's a hard trip—hard even for a man."

"If you can stand it I can," she assured him.

"But you don't belong in business of this sort. There'll be a crowd there—maybe trouble!"

"That's just why I'm going. You know what the feeling is against you. Do you think I'd let you go alone?"

"I don't intend to go in alone," she was surprised to hear him say. "I'm going to have Mr. Tracey send word to Furnace Creek. I'll have them and the South Fork men to back me up. Squaw Valley is going to the highest bidder—and I don't intend to be cheated out of it!"

Letty's face paled. If she had needed anything to confirm her fears, she had it now.

"There you are!" she exclaimed. "You've given yourself away! You wouldn't be drawing men in if you didn't expect trouble. I tell you, I'm going with you, Father!"

They were still arguing the matter when Judd and Tracey drove up in the rig.

"All right," he grumbled. "If you must go, get a heavy coat. It'll be right cold before sun-up."

CHAPTER II

"SAY WHAT YOU MEAN!"

A LITTLE knot of men stood grouped about the big map on the court-house steps. The land that was to be auctioned off was divided into quarter sections of one hundred and sixty acres. They spoke among themselves, a conscious restraint in their manner. Under the cottonwoods on the court-house lawn, other men waited, tall, lanky, their faces seamed and tanned in the way of desert men. There was a twang to their speech not unlike what one hears in the mountains of Kentucky. It was natural, for these men, or their fathers before them, had come from Kentucky and Tennessee, a hard-fighting race of pioneers who had been breaking the wilderness for generations.

There was a holiday air about their plain clothes; the occasion was important enough to warrant that. From time to time, one or the other would glance at his watch.

Jim Montana, seated at his desk in his office on the second floor, turned from watching them to glance at the clock on the wall. It was only eleven-thirty; half an hour yet before the sale would begin.

The tension that so obviously rested on the men

below found an echo in him. There was a set look about his strong mouth, the little laugh lines in the corners straight and uncompromising. His lean jaw, determined enough at any time, jutted out severely.

"No sign of trouble yet," he mused. "Maybe I'm going to get away with this after all . . . It won't take long."

Wild Horse was a one-street town. The court-house stood at one end of it. From where he sat, Montana commanded a view of it. There were very few vacant places at the hitchracks in front of the stores and saloons. Saddled horses and rigs of one sort or another lined both sides of the streets. It was Saturday. That always brought people to town. But this was like the Fourth of July. Some men had brought their families with them—women and children to whom even such a place as Wild Horse held excitement and diversion.

Montana had grown up on a ranch; he could appreciate the interest with which three sun-browned boys were regarding the articles on display in the window of Charlie Brown's hardware store.

"This thing to-day is going to mean a lot to them later on—school and better clothes," he thought.

Across the street an Indian stalked out of the tiny frame shack that served Clay Quantrell as an office for his freight and express business. Montana recognized him. It was young Plenty Eagles. He was not a reservation Indian. Since the snow had gone off that spring, he had been teaming for Quantrell between Wild Horse and the Jordan River Country.

Quantrell came to the door a moment later and called to the Indian, but Plenty Eagles only walked faster. He was making directly for the entrance to the court-house, and it was easy to see that he was enraged over something.

"Looks like a bad day all around for our red brothers," Jim thought aloud. He shook his head sadly. His sympathy was all with them. He toyed with the freshly stamped letter that lay on his desk. It contained his resignation. He knew forces would be brought to bear against him for what he was doing to-day that would make his dismissal certain. The resignation was just his way of beating those forces to the draw.

He did not regret the stand he was taking. It would make him enemies as well as friends. That seemed rather unimportant just now. "A man's got to play his cards according to the way they're dealt to him," he thought.

Someone was clumping up the stairs. The door of his office stood open. A moment later, Plenty Eagles stamped in. Clay Quantrell was only a step behind him.

Plenty Eagles was tall for a Piute. He brought a great excitement into the room with him, his piercing black eyes smoking with rage.

Jim knew him well. He raised his hand and gave him the sign. "How, *Cola!*"

Plenty Eagles drew himself up stiffly. "No! Long time I am knowing you. When you work for Henry Stall, many times I am come to your camp. Always you spread the robe for me and call me brother. I am trusting you. *Aiee!*" He pulled down the corners of his mouth with withering contempt. "Your tongue is crooked! It says one thing and means another!"

Montana looked to Quantrell for the answer to all this.

"Don't pay any attention to him, Jim," Quantrell said, trying to make light of the matter. "I tried to talk to him, but he wouldn't listen. He thinks you are driving his people off the reservation."

"My father old man; he not like leaving reservation," Plenty Eagles exclaimed fiercely. "Squaw Valley good place, he say. Indians living there long time. Not go away. All the time be sad for these hills."

Quantrell found a chair and sprawled all over it. "Did you ever hear anythin' sillier?" he laughed again.

His derision rubbed Montana the wrong way. They were not the cronies Quantrell liked to pretend they were, although of late he had been spending a lot of time in Jim's office.

"Nothing very funny about this to me," Montana said coolly. "Plenty Eagles is right; it's a damned nasty business yanking his people out of Squaw Valley. When they consented to go there they were led to believe the valley would be theirs forever. Now some fathead in Washington has discovered the Government can save a few dollars by packing them off to Fort Hall." He turned to the Indian. "You bet it's pretty tough, Plenty Eagles. You tell your father my heart bleeds for him. I love these hills, too."

"Then why you make him go?"

"I not make him go," Montana answered with great patience. "Letter comes; says Piutes go to Fort Hall; sell reservation. Men in Washington do this—not me."

"Sure, Plenty Eagles! You got this all wrong," Quantrell cut in, his face an emotionless mask even as he grinned, his teeth white against his swarthy skin. "Jim didn't have anything to do with it. When the soldiers come up from Fort McDermitt next month to move your folks, they'll go peaceful enough. They'll have to go; ain't nothing else for 'em to do. Better hitch up your team and pull out; you got a heavy load."

Jim knew Plenty Eagles had not been listening to Quantrell. There was a puzzled look on the Indian's face.

"You put up plenty sign about sell reservation," said he. "I show him to Quantrell. He say, 'Take down those signs; Montana not have sale.' Me, I tear them up. Now you have sale anyhow."

If Quantrell was surprised or annoyed by Plenty Eagles' admission that he had destroyed the legal notices of the sale, he gave no sign of it.

"Did you tell him that, Clay?" Jim asked, pushing back his chair as though to get to his feet. Quantrell waved him down.

"Don't be foolish!" he drawled. "He just got me wrong, that's all. I—happen to know they can send you to prison for tearing up them things." He lit a cigarette and blew a cloud of smoke in the Indian's direction. "Plenty Eagles, I wouldn't go around repeating what you just said. It might get you into trouble."

The baffled look deepened in the Piute's eyes. He sensed that there was a game here, but he couldn't understand it. Prison? He understood that perfectly. His face remained immobile and stern, but his shoulders sagged impotently; he had been tricked before. Without another word he shuffled out of the office and went down the stairs.

Quantrell smoked his cigarette unconcernedly. He knew Montana was regarding him thoughtfully. An impudent smile parted his lips. "Don't pretend you're surprised," he purred. "You knew the signs were down. You did your duty; you put 'em up. If they didn't stay up, you should worry. It served your purpose as well as mine."

"Yeah?" Montana's blue eyes were cold and gray. "You're pretty sure I've got a purpose, eh?"

"I hope to tell you I am!" Quantrell began to lose some of the nonchalance he liked to affect as Montana continued to regard him. "I got your play right off. You want to freeze old Slick-ear out of Squaw Valley." Quantrell permitted himself another smile. "Feeling the same way about it, I began to sit up nights, figuring out ways to help you."

"When I need help I usually know how to ask for it."
Jim's tone was definitely hostile. "Why are you so
interested?"

"That's a fair question," Quantrell replied bluntly.
"I'll give you a fair answer. Half of my business has
been freighting Government issues to the agency in
Squaw Valley. That's all over now. But if you can't
make a living one way, you got to do it another. God
knows that ranch of mine will never put a dollar in my
pocket as it stands. My only out is to buy in some of
this reservation bottom land, so I'll have hay and water
and make it a going concern. I'm chucking the freighting business."

"Oh . . . "

"I guess you know now why I don't want Henry
Stall poking his nose into Squaw Valley and gobbling
up the whole damn works." Quantrell hitched his chair
nearer to the desk and leaned forward confidentially.
"Seeing the conversation has taken this turn, Jim," he
ran on, "reminds me of something. Section number
seven—just above the forks—is what I got my eye on.
You can—fix things so I'll get it, can't you?"

The silence that followed grew oppressive. Quantrell
began to fidget as Jim's eyes burned into his.

"Clay—I ought to kick you out of here for that,"
he said at last. "You talk as though you had something
on me. If you have—shoot! I'm not fixing anything
for anybody."

"Of course not!" Quantrell knew he had overstepped himself. "All I meant was—if you can give me a break, why—I'll appreciate it."

"Well, you want to say what you mean with me," Montana flung back. He pulled himself erect and walked over to the window and gazed up and down the street. Plenty Eagles was pulling out of town with his twelve-mule team.

Only the droning of the flies, sailing in and out of the unscreened window, and the ticking of the clock on the wall broke the silence as Quantrell rolled another cigarette. As he moistened the paper with his tongue, he raised his eyes to flash a glance of hatred at Montana's back. "I'll square that some day," he promised himself.

Jim's eyes had strayed to the road that led into town from the southwest. Quantrell saw him stiffen. He failed to surmise the reason.

"Well, only a few minutes now and you can get started," he drawled. "All the interested parties are present."

"Yes—thanks to you!" Jim whipped out.

Quantrell caught the challenge in his voice. "What do you mean?" he demanded as Jim whirled on him.

"Judd Case was in here yesterday morning. Said you'd been talking to him."

Quantrell flushed. "No use denying it," he got out awkwardly. "Just razzing him a little. It was too late to do any harm."

"I might have known it," Montana ground out

furiously. "You had to play the tin-horn, didn't you?"

"Say, *muchacho*, I don't intend to eat all the dust you kick up!" Quantrell towered above Montana as they faced each other, his mouth cruel and reckless.

"Take a look out the window," Jim muttered.

A dozen men were riding into town. They were armed—alert and unfriendly. Quantrell let a grunt of dismay escape him.

"You know them?" Montana rasped unpleasantly.

"Reb Russell and the Bar S bunch from Furnace Creek!" The big fellow's voice trailed away to a smothered whisper.

"Look the other way—beyond the tracks. See anything?"

"My God!" was Quantrell's answering exclamation.

"Yeah! Too late to do any harm, eh? You ought to grow up, Quantrell. This'll be the old man himself and his South Fork outfit. They're not here by accident."

Downstairs the hum of conversation fell away to an excited whisper. The sober faces of the men who had been waiting about the court-house grew graver as they recognized Reb and his men. They drew together, silent and tight of lip. Suddenly the very air had become charged with a breathless tension.

Quantrell's air of confidence had vanished when he turned away from the window, "It's a show-down now," he got out. "Are you going through with your play?"

"I haven't any play left," Montana answered stonily. "A tin-horn kicked my hand into the discard."

Quantrell reared up defiantly, his face white with rage.

"Get going!" Montana warned. "When that crowd downstairs learns the right of this they'll be looking for you with a rope!"

CHAPTER III

TO THE HIGHEST BIDDER

BACK in the beginning, when the rape of the West began, the universal intention of cattleman and miner had been to rip out a fortune in a hurry. Nobody was concerned about the land or its future. That was still the thought when Henry Stall, a German butcher-boy, come to California to make his fortune, first set foot in San Francisco.

Frugal and industrious, he proved an apt pupil. Fifteen years later, men were calling him the cattle-king as he journeyed up and down the San Joaquin, his note-book in his pocket. It was his own domain; his by right of conquest.

"On March 16th, and again a week later, seated in a rowboat, we travelled back and forth across the area herein described," two of his men made sworn affidavit to the U. S. Land Office in an action looking toward the acquiring of still more land. The two men were in the rowboat, as they testified; but they failed to state that the rowboat had been lashed to a wagon and that a team of horses had drawn them over the land in question. It was typical of Henry Stall.

With his chain-store mind and mania for expansion,

it was inevitable that he should invade Nevada and later, Oregon. In this semi-desert country there was an abundance of range, but precious little water. Immediately, he began to prospect for it, filing on every creek and spring he found unused, making them his own by the simple expedient of proving his priority and a real or fancied use of the waters in question. Once established, those rights were his forever, and he foresaw that through them he would dominate this country sooner or later even as he did the San Joaquin.

That thought had been in his mind the August day he first rode into Squaw Valley. Other than the reservation, it was all uninhabited public domain, open to entry. With dummy entrymen he could have homesteaded most of it, or bought it in for the proverbial song. He was not minded to do either, for without the reservation there was not enough good range in sight to interest him. It satisfied him to buy a few scattered acres and establish what water rights he could.

In the twelve years that had intervened, one small outfit after another had moved into the valley, using water that he considered his. He made no protest, willing to bide his time until such a day as this arrived. He knew the passing years had not outlawed his rights —not with the legal talent he could send to the firing line. Those old water rights were an ace in the hole now.

If he rode into Wild Horse outwardly his usual phlegmatic self, he was aware of the hostile glances levelled at him. It was no more than he expected. In the crowd he recognized Dan Crockett, Joe Gault and one or two others.

"I don't want to be hard on these Squaw Valley men," he said to himself. "If I get the reservation, I'll buy them out at a fair price." His idea of a fair price, of course. "But they can't expect to use my water if they band together and try to freeze me out."

He rode ahead with Letty and Judd. A dozen South Fork men followed close behind.

"Reb's here already," Judd informed him as they neared the court-house. "Over there in front of the sheriff's office."

"So I see." The old man glanced at his watch. It was five minutes to twelve. "I'm going up and talk to Montana before the sale starts. You tell Mr. Russell I don't want any trouble if it can be avoided.

Letty sighed wearily as she slipped from her saddle. The long, gruelling ride had told on her more than on her father.

"You better stay here with Mr. Case," he advised.

"No, I'll go up with you," she insisted. "It won't look so warlike if I go along."

Montana expected the old man to come up. He was surprised to find Letty with him. It was the first time he had seen her in more than a year—a period in which he had tried unsuccessfully to keep memory of her out of his thoughts.

His belated "Good-morning," won no response from old Henry. Letty nodded, her manner cool and aloof and in marked contrast to the warm friendliness of the days when he had been a Bar S man.

It hurt; but he told himself he could expect nothing else under the circumstances. She refused the chair he offered her.

"I thought you were going to keep me posted about this matter," old Slick-ear queried without preamble of any sort.

"I changed my mind about that, Mr. Stall," Montana answered with equal bluntness. "I don't mind telling you I am sorry to see you here."

That was direct enough. The old man drew down his shaggy eyebrows.

"Your gratitude for the good wages I paid you for three years, eh?"

"You may not believe it, but gratitude had something to do with it—though I aim to be worthy of my hire. I never heard anyone accuse you of overpaying a man."

It was a pertinent shot. Letty had difficulty keeping a twinkle out of her eyes as she saw her father's head go up indignantly.

"You are entitled to your opinion," he exclaimed sharply. "But you haven't any right to discriminate against me."

"Neither against nor for you," Montana supplemented.

It nettled the old man to be rebuffed so completely.

"I didn't come here to bandy words with you! The facts speak for themselves. When a man goes to all the bother you have about something that doesn't concern him, I begin to wonder what he's getting out of it."

Jim refused to lose his temper.

"I suppose you mean I may be trying to feather my own nest," he said. "All I hoped to do was pull out of this with a clean conscience. But I won't try to disabuse your mind on that. You think what you please."

"You can't deny your conduct has been very—irregular, to say the least."

"Possibly irregular, but not illegal, Mr. Stall. I have been careful about that."

"Agents have been removed for less."

The threat failed to have the desired effect. Jim tapped the letter on his desk.

"I have already removed myself," he said grimly. "I'll be looking for a job next month."

Letty could not help feeling that her father was coming off second best in this tilt of words. He nervously fingered the heavy gold watch chain that spanned his vest as he tried to dissemble his rage.

"A smart Aleck gets a little authority and disrupts a whole county," he grumbled. "Your meddling is bound to cause trouble."

"I am sorry if that is so," Jim said thoughtfully. "It's been the one thing I wanted to avoid. You're a rich man, Mr. Stall. You don't need an acre of this Squaw Valley land. But take Morrow, or Gault, or Dan Crockett—a dozen others—what have they got? They're just getting by, that's all. Beef is down; it's been a dry spring. They won't make hay enough to carry them through next winter. I figured if they could borrow from the bank and pick up some of this reservation they'd get enough water and bottom land to see 'em through. It wouldn't make any of them rich, but it would put them on their feet."

This appeal to his sympathy fell on deaf ears, as Jim expected.

"I'm sorry," the old man said, "but you can't expect me to wet-nurse the cattle business. Nobody ever helped me; what I've got I got for myself. All I can do to take care of my own business."

"Exactly! And it will be your business to run every one of these little fellows out of Squaw Valley. I know how you work."

Anger began to run away with the old man. "What do you mean by that?" he demanded indignantly.

Jim's answer was unhurried.

"I think you know what I mean, Mr. Stall. I happened to discover that you filed on most of the water over there years ago. Soon as you get the reservation, you'll go to court and prove up on those rights. It will be the beginning of the end for the little fellows. They'll have some range, but you'll have their water, and they can do one of two things: Move on without a dime, or sell out to you at your own terms."

The charge left old Slick-ear speechless for a moment. His stubby mustache bristled like the quills on a porcupine's back.

Letty put an arm about him protectively. The blood had drained away from her cheeks.

"Father—don't bother to answer anything as absurd as that! You've always been fair—more than fair—" She whirled on Montana fiercely. "I never thought you could be that contemptible."

He had never seen her like that before, superb in her indignation. And yet, he knew he had voiced only the truth.

"I'm sorry you had to hear that," he said unhappily. "You shouldn't have come."

"I'm glad I came! It's been very—enlightening."

The clock was striking twelve. Old Henry reached for his hat.

"Come on, Letty; we'll go downstairs. It's time for the sale to begin." He turned to Montana for a parting shot. "I let those people use my water for twelve years so you can accuse me of wanting to drive them out, eh? Well, I'm here, and I didn't come alone. I don't intend to be intimidated."

"Neither do I, Mr. Stall. I haven't any paid warriors to back me up, but if I knew how to keep you from grabbing Squaw Valley I'd do it."

"If you knew how, eh?" Old Slick-ear's voice dripped with contempt. "You won't have much to do about it, Montana. This is not my first land sale. You'll run it off according to the rules of the Land Office. The property will go to the highest bidder!"

He started for the door. Letty followed him, her

chin held high. Clearer than words it told Montana in what contempt she held him. A tortured look in his eyes, he stared after her until she disappeared down the stairs.

"I guess that's final enough," he mused bitterly. "Can't blame her for stringing along with her father."

He had always regarded his affection for Letty Stall as hopeless. Nothing else had led him to leave the Bar S at a time when it was apparent the old man would have made him foreman of one of his ranches in a few months.

Memories of pleasant days with her at the Willow Vista ranch smote him. It made him realize that even in his hopelessness he had never quite ceased to hope.

Everything about this business seemed to have gone wrong.

"Maybe it will bring me to my senses," he thought, appalled anew by the absurdity of daring to aspire to her. Wealth, position—everything removed her from his world.

It occurred to him that he might advance his own interests by trying to placate her father.

"No, I can't do that. He's wrong about this, and I'm right, even though he's got me at the end of a limb."

This sale was the first one of importance that he had conducted. From a desk drawer he drew out his instructions and scanned them hastily. He had read them a score of times and knew them almost by heart. If Mr. Stall or anyone else wished to bid on the land as a whole, he would have to take the bid. He glanced over the terms under which the land might be sold, looking for a loophole or technicality he might invoke to defeat the old man even now.

As he was about to toss the letter back into his desk an idea flashed in his mind that pulled him up short. It intrigued him more the longer he considered it.

"If he does what I think he'll do, it'll be up to me to say yes or no," he murmured aloud in his abstraction. "It's Saturday—the bank is closed! He wouldn't have an out!"

He failed to hear someone run up the stairs. It was Clem Harvey, his surveyor. There was always something breathless about Clem, as though he didn't quite expect to finish what he had to say.

"Gee willikens, Jim," he exclaimed excitedly, "don't you know it's twelve o'clock? Everybody's waiting and people are beginning to get restless and——"

"I'm coming."

Montana's preoccupation caused Clem to push back his tattered Stetson and cock his head at him inquisitively.

"Ain't nothin' wrong is there? Ain't nothin'——"

"No, everything is all right, Clem." Jim's voice was hard and chilling. "Don't you hear the birds singing?"

"Birds?" A baffled look crept into Clem's watery eyes.

"Yeah, buzzards!...Come on, Let's go!"

CHAPTER IV

THE LETTER OF THE LAW

A GREAT hush rested on the crowd below. The Squaw Valley men had drawn apart, their faces grave. Their wives stood with them now, their shopping done—women old before their time with the never-ending drudgery that is a ranch-woman's life.

Man and wife, they resented Henry Stall's presence there. In him they recognized their common enemy, come to dash the cup of hope from their hands even as they were raising it to their lips. Because they came of a race of stout-hearted fighting men, even hopelessness could not strike fear in their hearts, and as they faced old Slick-ear and his men, lounging in the shade at the side of the sheriff's office, there was a smouldering defiance in their eyes and the set of their mouths that said they would not bow their heads to any oppressor.

Their hostility included Letty as well as her father. The fineness of her clothes, her air of self-possession embittered them. She felt it, too. It was as though she had wronged them. It made her wonder how much truth there was in what Montana had said. Upstairs, she had championed her father's cause and said he was

43

always fair. In her heart, she knew he could be ruthless, brooking no opposition when he'd set his mind on something.

Under a spreading box-elder, just beyond the steps, a young woman was trying to get her baby to sleep. Three other children, the oldest not over six, hovered about her, their eyes big and staring.

The girl was not much older than Letty, but already there was a pinched, hunted look in her eyes. There was something proud and defiant about her that made one forget her shabby clothes and hands, red and rough from hard work.

"Just getting by," Montana had said. The words came back to Letty, and she felt her heart go out to the woman. Impulsively she tried to caress the oldest child, a boy. He drew back, afraid. His mother caught him by the arm and drew him to her side.

"You stay right here, Jess," she scolded. "I don't want you takin' up with no strangers."

Letty turned away, pretending not to have heard. But everywhere she looked she met the same distrust and hostility. She knew their enmity was not personal to her; she was a stranger to them. But she was her father's daughter, and they hated her accordingly. It drove home the realization that for all his talk of fair-play, the business about to be enacted had an ugly side.

Montana came out then. The charged silence deepened as he walked over to the big map. His manner was solemn. Letty thought he seemed embarrassed at finding himself the center of attention.

"If you'll step nearer, we'll begin," he said.

Quantrell, tall and saturnine, stood with the Squaw Valley men. He moved forward and the others followed him. Old Slick-ear mounted the steps alone, unabashed by the glances levelled at him.

Montana read the letter authorizing the sale.

"The land will be sold to the highest bidder," he went on. "The terms: twenty-five per cent now and the balance when title is given." He turned and pointed to the map. "The map has been divided into quarter sections. I cannot accept a bid for any parcel less than one hundred and sixty acres. I will begin the sale with section one, offering it first as a whole section. Are there any offers?"

"Just a minute, Montana," Old Henry interrupted. "You are authorized to accept bids on this property as a whole."

It was the very thing Montana had been waiting for him to say.

"That's correct," he admitted, his tone guileless. "If anybody cares to make a bid on the reservation as a whole I am compelled to accept that bid."

An angry murmur broke from the Squaw Valley men. They knew Montana and regarded him as their friend. They had not expected him to sell them out without a protest.

"Are there any bids on the property as a whole?"

"Three dollars an acre!" Old Slick-ear clipped the words off short.

"A man can't come in here and hog it like that!" Quantrell burst out angrily. "Where do we come in, Montana?"

"You're right, Quantrell! We don't aim to be cheated like that!" It was Dan Crockett. The other Squaw Valley men rallied about him instantly.

Montana continued to gaze at the old man.

"That's the minimum bid, Mr. Stall," he said. "It's a ridiculous price."

"It's my bid!"

The Bar S men had got to their feet and drawn closer. Over their heads came the creaking of leather as the horses fought the flies.

"The law compels me to accept it," Jim droned tonelessly. "Are there any other bids?"

Dan Crockett stepped up to him, his face grim and determined.

"There's going to be trouble here, Montana, if you go through with this," he warned. "We all thought you was our friend."

"I am your friend, Dan, but my hands are tied; I've got to take this bid. If there's any trouble here, don't you start it." He raised his voice. "Are there any other bids?"

There were none.

"Sold to Stall and Matlack!"

It was a moment pregnant with tragedy. There were

a hundred armed men in that crowd. It needed only a word to start the conflagration.

Quantrell was beside himself. In the emergency, he elected to become the self-appointed leader of the Squaw Valley faction. Crockett and the others were too stunned by the sudden turn of events to object.

"It ain't no more than you'd expect from a man who'd let an Indian call him a liar and get away with it," he bellowed as he started up the steps.

Montana kept his head. A few seconds now would tell the tale. The form he was filling out was about ready. Quantrell pushed in between him and the old man.

"There'll be blood spilled here if you go through with this, Montana," he spit out threateningly.

"And there'll be a lynching as well as a land sale," Jim murmured calmly as he finished the form. "If you think I'm bluffing—call my hand."

Implacable hatred blazed in Quantrell's eyes. He wanted to go through with the play he had started, but wisdom warned him that the very men who were backing him up now would be the first to turn against him if they learned that it was his babbling that had wrecked their hopes.

Old Slick-ear thought he understood Montana's answer; but it was no affair of his. He had won easier than he expected, and he was content. He looked the form over. It was in order. He got out a pencil and made some figures on the back of his notebook.

"Twenty-five per cent will be eight thousand, two hundred dollars—right?"

"That's right, Mr. Stall," Jim agreed. "Eight thousand, two hundred dollars."

The old man brought out a Stall and Matlack scriptbook as well-known as money in that country. Wages, bills, taxes—every Stall and Matlack transaction was paid in that familiar green script with the bull's head adorning it.

"If you'll step up to your office," he said, "I'll fill out this script."

The moment had arrived. Jim shook his head. The eyes of the crowd were on them.

"I'm sorry, Mr. Stall," he declared thoughtfully, "but I can't take your script."

"You can't take it? What do you mean you can't take it?"

"The terms of this sale are cash."

"Cash?" Old Slick-ear's face was purple with rage. "My script's as good as cash! Any bank will take it. The government recognizes it as legal tender."

The crowd had quickly sensed that something was amiss. They swarmed up the steps, the Bar S men alert and the others on guard.

"You're not quite right about that. The government has accepted your script as legal tender, but it has never expressly recognized it as such."

"Say, don't be a damned fool, Montana!" Reb Russell exclaimed angrily. "You know the Bar S script is as good as cash. We ain't goin' to let you get away with any nonsense like that."

Jim was well acquainted with the freckle-faced foreman of Furnace Creek.

"Listen, Reb," he said, and his voice was velvety, "I got an awful idea you're trying to force my hand. If that's the case, you'd better forget it. You ought to know by this time that I don't bluff worth a cent. My business is with Mr. Stall—and it's almost finished." He turned to the old man again. "You insisted on the full letter of the law. Now it's my turn. I know your script is all right; but it isn't cash, and I refuse to accept it."

A cheer arose from the Squaw Valley men. Even Quantrell dared to join in it.

"Why, you young fool, I'll run you out of the country for this!" old Slick-ear roared. "There's courts in this state that will protect me. I bought this land in good faith, and I want my rights."

"You're getting your rights, the same as any other man here."

"Well, give me ten minutes then. I'll make Longyear open the bank. He'll cash my script."

"I won't give you one minute, Mr. Stall!" Montana answered unhesitatingly. "I told you upstairs I would do anything I could to keep you out of Squaw Valley. I meant it . . . The sale will go on!"

"You idiot, you!" the old man trembled as though he had the palsy. "Do you realize what you're doing?"

"I think I do," Jim answered tensely.

"I don't think so! You talk about befriending these people. I warn you you'll never do it this way. The minute the courts recognize my rights in Squaw Valley, I'm moving in—and I'm moving in to stay! You're forcing a war to the finish on all of us!"

"That may be," Jim admitted. "God knows they'd rather go down fighting than wait for you to crush them." He picked up his yardstick again. "The sale will continue!" he cried. "Section one, the northeast quarter! What am I bid?"

Joe Tracey, Judd Case and Reb gathered about the old man and Letty.

"The sale won't go on if you want it stopped," Reb informed him. "We can stampede this crowd."

The old man was biting his mustache nervously. For once he seemed not to know his own mind.

"Father—we're going!" Letty exclaimed. "I can't stand any more of this!" She got her arm around his. "Please——"

"Might as well," he decided grudgingly. "I'll fight this in my own way. We'll let this smart aleck have his little party to-day."

If Montana noticed that the Bar S was leaving en masse, he gave no sign of it. The sale proceeded satisfactorily. Everybody seemed to get what they wanted, except Quantrell. He had to be satisfied with half a loaf. But prices were cheap, the land good. They knew they'd never give it up without a struggle.

Finding himself near a post-office, old Slick-ear had to tarry to write his usual stack of letters, included in which were his voluminous epistles to his foremen, apprising them when and where to meet him, or not to expect him at all, and going into the minutest details about a hundred things he expected them to take care of before he should next see them.

By the time he had finished, he had so far recovered his temper as to suggest that they have dinner before starting their long ride back to the South Fork and Willow Vista.

Letty had no desire for food, but to humor him, she accompanied him to the dining-room of the hotel. He ate as slowly and methodically as he did everything else. Busy with his thoughts, he kept his eyes on his plate as he munched his food, and said nothing. Letty was equally engrossed in her own musing.

They had almost finished when he surprised her by saying:

"I made a mistake in not making Montana a foreman last year. There wouldn't have been any of this nonsense to-day if I had. But like as not he would have done something else just as foolish. A man that can't mind his own business isn't worth his salt. He certainly made a spectacle of himself to-day, the contemptible ingrate!"

"Not to me," Letty murmured tremulously, her eyes fixed on the crowd moving away from the court-house. "I—I thought he was magnificent."

CHAPTER V

BACKS TO THE WALL

POETS have made immortal the exile of the humble Acadian farmers from the homes and the land they loved. The Squaw Valley Piutes had no poet to sing their swan song. But their passing was hardly less tragic. For countless generations they had waged incessant warfare against their natural enemies, the Bannocks and the Snakes, for the land of their fathers. They had even waged a long and losing fight against their white brothers. A remnant of a once proud race, they had consented to be herded together in Squaw Valley. Now even that last refuge had been taken from them.

For fifty years a benign government had said in effect that one reservation was as good as another for an Indian. What difference could it possibly make to him where he found himself? Fort Hall was a big reservation. Three hundred Piutes would not overcrowd it. Of course it was a Bannock reservation. But what of that?

Debauched, exploited, mute—perhaps it was strange that it could matter, that the blood hatred of a Piute for a Bannock still coursed through their veins.

Old men and women, children—a troop of cavalry hurrying them along—they filed into Wild Horse, their worldly goods piled hit or miss on a long line of army wagons. In the truest sense, they all were children, with a child's eagerness to be amused. Ordinarily, a trip to Wild Horse would have been an adventure. But their eyes were dull to-day, their faces stolid.

"*Aie-e-e, aiee,*" the old squaws wailed as they called on Nanibashoo, the god of their fathers, to help them.

Little Boy, their tribal chief, a wrinkled and toothless old man, rode on the first wagon, proud and dignified, a chief even in his rags.

"*Aie-e-e,*" Montana echoed. He sat alone with Graham Rand, the sheriff, in the latter's tiny office. His face was stern. "They don't savvy this at all," he said. "When Little Boy saw me, I got his thought. They think I did this to them."

"They're crazy!" The sheriff drew his shaggy brows down. "They never had a better friend. You're all Indian under the skin, Jim."

"There's two of us. I reckon you'd throw that star away in a hurry if they'd only give us back this country as it used to be before the barbed wire hit it." Montana mused to himself for a moment. "Graham, I didn't see Thunder Bird in that bunch. Did you?"

The marshal grinned mischievously as he shook his head.

"I helped him to get away, Jim. He's hiding out in the old Adelaide mine on Quantrell's ranch. Plenty

Eagles asked me to do something; his father didn't want to leave the Malheurs. He'll have to lay low for a couple of weeks."

"He's too old to work," Montana thought aloud. "Plenty Eagles will have to take care of him."

"I'll see that he does," Rand volunteered. "The old fellow's got grub enough to last ten days." He paused to refill his pipe. "No need to tell you to say nothin' about this over there," he went on presently. "What you aimin' to do, Jim?"

"I'm going to strike Dan Crockett for a job."

"Yeah?" In the inflection of his voice there was deep understanding rather than surprise. "Gunnin' for trouble, eh?"

"No, just hoping I can steady the boat a little. The old man won't back up an inch, now that the courts have upheld him. He can do about as he pleases in that country. With Creiger and his deputies to help him, he'll take possession of his water."

"And when old Slick-ear puts on the pressure, something happens!" Graham summed up tersely. "The next thing he'll do will be to move in enough men and stock to worry that Squaw Valley crowd into doin' somethin' foolish."

"I expect he's moved in already." Montana's expression was as grave as his words. "Mr. Stall never wastes any time."

That night he camped on Skull Creek, inside of the

old reservation and several miles north of where the creek flows into the Malheur.

Imagine a great inverted capital V with the Malheur Range forming the eastern line and the Junipers the western. Picture the Malheur River, rising in the Junipers and flowing to the north and east, so as to close the great triangle, and you have Squaw Valley, with the reservation occupying the lower part of the triangle. To the north, extending into the mountains, you would find the eight and nine-thousand acre outfits that were fighting for existence.

There were three creeks of major importance in the valley. From east to west: Skull Creek, Big Powder Creek and Owl Creek. Eventually, all found their way to the Malheur.

Montana rolled his blankets at dawn. The valley was wide there, not less than twenty miles from range to range. The scene was a familiar one to him. Beyond the willows and aspens that choked the creek bottom, the native bluejoint grew high and green, even though the year was a dry one. Because sheep had never ranged there, no ugly patches of burr or broncho grass marred that blue-green expanse.

At that hour, the rolling Junipers to the west looked like great tufts of pink cotton. The Malheurs, nearer and more formidable, too, rose sheer and forbidding, varnished-green patches of mountain mahogany marking the spots where the snow lay late in the spring.

Skull Creek purled over the rocks at Montana's feet,

as garrulous as an old woman, as he waited for the coffee to boil.

"Just as sassy as usual," he said. "Think you'd get tired, jawing away like that night and day."

He had not finished breakfast when he caught the sound of breaking brush up the creek. Presently, two mounted troopers rode into view.

"Saw your smoke a long way off," said one. "We thought you might be the party we're lookin' for. But God knows you ain't an Injun."

From their conversation Jim surmised that they had made only a perfunctory search for Plenty Eagles' father. He invited them to share his flapjacks, but they said no.

"Goin' back to McDermitt, the younger of the two explained. "Want to get started before the sun begins to climb."

After they had gone on, Montana saddled his horse and followed the creek north. The afternoon was well along before he reached Dan Crockett's Box C ranch.

Dan, together with his cousins, the Gaults and the Morrows, had been the first to run cattle in the upper valley. He was thrifty and a hard worker, as were his grown sons. Comparatively, he had done well, but the Box C was a far cry from any one of the big Bar S ranches.

Dan was repairing a wagon-box as Montana rode into the yard.

"Hi, Jim!" he called out, surprised to see him there.

"What you all doin' up this way? You still workin' fer Uncle Sam?"

"No, I'm paying my own wages now," Montana laughed as he slid from his saddle. "And that's a condition that's got to be corrected awful sudden, Dan."

Crockett's habitually solemn face creased into a smile.

"Well, with all this war-talk in the air, there ain't no one I'd rather have around than you," he said. "A top hand is worth fifty a month and cakes. I ain't got no right to be treating myself to a luxury like that, but I reckon you're hired." His smile flickered out. "Things are goin' to happen fast around here, Jim. In fact they begun to happen already. The Bar S moved in yesterday."

"I reckoned they would," Montana acknowledged glumly. "They drive some stock in?"

"About five hundred head. They came in through the Malheurs from Furnace Creek. They're on the Big Powder and the North Fork of the Skull. There's at least twenty Bar S men with Reb."

"So Reb's going to represent for the old man, eh?" Montana shook his head slowly. "That ought to show you how things are drifting. If the old man wasn't looking for trouble he'd have given this job to Joe Tracey or Case—somebody who'd be awfully slow on the draw. Reb's distinctly hair-trigger . . . Did anything happen?"

"Not so far as I know. It looked like trespassing to

move across a man's range; but the sheriff was here, spoutin' law. He says a man's got a right to move his stuff up to his own water. The boys let it go at that. Quantrell was there. He's a fire-eater; you know that. His talk sounded good to some, I reckon. But Dave Morrow and Gault and me cooled them down."

"Quantrell hasn't any judgment," Montana declared bluntly. "Look out for him, Dan; he's a trouble maker. The old man is going to give us every chance to overplay our hand. If we do, look out! He can move two hundred men in here. And the law will ride with 'em, 'cause he can deputize every one of them!"

"I know it," Dan nodded. "You ain't paintin' it any blacker than it is. With Furnace Creek on the east and Willow Vista to the southwest, he can squeeze us on two sides—and he will, Jim. I reckon until last week he didn't have a thousand acres in the valley—and that was cut up into four pieces. He's got more now."

"Where'd he get it?" Montana asked uneasily.

Dan squatted on his toes and began to draw a map on the ground.

"You can see the old Adelaide mine from here," he explained. "Quantrell's line goes north of there about two miles." He indicated it with his stick. "From there, right through the Junipers to the Willow Vista line, was Eph Mellon's range . . . You follow me, Montana?"

"Yes. And——?"

Dan tossed away his stick and stood up.

"Eph sold out to the Bar S on Monday," he muttered gloomily. "Old Slick-ear's line is now right here in the valley. He's driven a wedge right into the middle of us—and you'll see plenty Bar S steers in here before you git your hair cut ag'in."

Montana did not try to hide his vexation. By advancing the boundary line of Willow Vista into the very heart of Squaw Valley, the Bar S had scored a tactical victory that strengthened their stand immeasurably. He could appreciate the fortitude it took to face the future calmly.

Gene and Brent Crockett, Dan's sons, narrow-hipped six-footers, rode in half an hour later. Both were taciturn, in the way of the mountain breed. If they were surprised to see Montana, they dissembled it.

"The boys have been movin' some of our stuff onto our new range in the reservation," Dan explained. "Without the North Fork water I can't keep 'em up here no longer. Course I'm better off than some folks. I had some water rights of my own that the Bar S couldn't grab. But you know how range cattle are, Jim. They get used to waterin' in one place and they'll go back to it in spite of hell. That's where the rub is goin' to come. I suggested to Reb that we put up a line fence and each pay half of the cost."

"I don't suppose that interested him," Montana volunteered. "That's not the Bar S game."

"No, he wouldn't lissen at all. Said he'd keep his stuff on his own range and we'd have to do the same."

"Darin' us, that's all!" Gene Crockett muttered bitterly. He was the younger of the two boys. "It's a fine law that lets an outfit rob you like that! That water was our'n. Mebbe old man Stall saw it 'fore Pap did. That didn't make it his if he didn't use it. We ain't no better off than we was 'fore they opened up the reservation. Now we got water in one place and range in another, and nothin' short o' God a'mighty can make a steer eat one place and drink another."

"No use losin' your haid about it," his father protested. "We got to go easy and figure this thing out."

"It's all right to talk about takin' things easy, Pap," the other boy declared soberly, "but Gene's right; you can't swallow everythin' they hand you and pretend to like it. I hazed a cow and her calf out of the North Fork bottoms for over an hour this morning. Like as not she's back there right now. That's what the Bar S wants. They'll catch our stuff trespassing and using their water. Lawsuits will be slapped on us till we're busted. Then we can git out."

"You said it!" Gene agreed. "Clay Quantrell's got the right idea. If we're goin' to git licked anyhow, let's git licked fightin'! Why wait 'til we're helpless?"

Montana had known the boys for years. Their bitterness was no surprise, but he had expected them to be long-suffering rather than rash under the first prod of the Bar S. Their talk sounded reckless. Since Quantrell's name had come into the conversation, Montana thought he had the explanation.

"That's brave talk, Gene," he said, "but I'm afraid it won't get us anywhere. We can't shoot this thing out and win. If we want to beat that bunch we've got to outsmart them."

The boys were not impressed with his logic, but their father agreed with him.

"There can't be any doubt of it," he said with great deliberation. "Spillin' a lot of blood won't settle this at all. The first thing we got to do is get organized. We're goin' to have a meetin' here towards evenin'. I reckon most of the folks will come." He glanced at the westering sun. "Gene will take you over to the house and show you where to drop your war-bag. We'll have supper before the crowd comes."

CHAPTER VI

TRAGEDY RIDES THE RANGE

IN ADDITION to his sons, Dan had two men on the ranch,—Romero, the Mexican, and Ben Vining, an old-time buckaroo from Nevada. They ate together in the ranch kitchen, Mrs. Crockett doing the cooking.

Eating was a solemn rite that seemed to dry up the wells of conversation.

Before they had finished, people began to arrive. With one or two exceptions they were all related in some way to the Crocketts.

"One or two others to come yet," Dan told them. "We'll wait a few minutes."

Quantrell was the last to arrive. He gave Jim a curt nod. His displeasure was evident on learning that Montana had injected himself into the fight and was now riding for the Box C. He had an excuse for his tardiness. Jim thought his horse looked as though it had been ridden hard.

The meeting got under way at last . . . The day had been one to try tempers. A dozen men recounted their verbal clashes with Reb and his men. All agreed that they must stand together.

Dan Crockett spoke at length, advising them to be

patient and stay within the law. They listened, but there was no enthusiasm for what he had to say.

Quantrell spoke, fanning their hatred of the Bar S.

"The law's too one-sided for me!" he bellowed. "The other fellow's got it all! We got to take care of this in our own way—without the help of any outsiders!"

Evidently it was what they wanted to hear, for they cheered him when he finished. Montana knew this reference to outsiders was directed at him. He couldn't escape the feeling that the fight was resolving itself into a personal one between Quantrell and himself. His face was stern and uncompromising as he arose and faced them.

"I want to remind you men that when anybody labels me an outsider that you consider the facts," he began. "I saw this trouble coming long before any of you gave it a thought. If Henry Stall had got the reservation—where would you be now?"

"We'd be on our way out!" Dan exclaimed courageously. "There ain't a man here but has to thank you for what you did, Montana."

There was muttered approval of this, in which Quantrell did not join. He leaned on the corral gate with sullen defiance in his eyes.

"Well, if I was with you then, I'm with you now," Montana continued. "And I'm with you all the way. Loose talk almost cost you the reservation—the same sort of talk that refers to me now as an outsider." His eyes were fixed on Quantrell. A sneer curled the big fellow's mouth. "You've been told that the law was all on the other fellow's side. It's true. And it's the best reason I know for staying clear of it. You've got your homes here. You've got to think of your wives and children. Blood won't help them."

He paused to let the effect of his words sink in.

"This fight has just begun, and yet, your patience is gone already. You can't win that way! My God, men, where is the iron in you? You haven't lost yet! Don't let yourselves be stampeded into taking the law into your own hands!"

Lance Morrow stepped into the cleared space in front of Jim. He was a little bandy-legged man, nearing seventy, and the father of five strapping sons.

"Montana, I was nursed on a rifle. I've lived with one all my life, but I was taught never to take hit down unless I couldn't git justice no other way. I don't want to take hit down now. My boys feel as I do about hit. But what are we agoin' to do, Montana? Man to man, what hope have we got?"

The old man had put it concretely. That was what they all wanted to know; what hope did they have? They waited anxiously for Montana to answer.

Jim refused to be hurried.

"Well," he said at last, "I never knew Henry Stall to send bad dollars after good ones when time had proved that he had a losing proposition on his hands. If you stand pat and stick together, you can beat him.

He can't consolidate his water unless some one of you sells him land. The man who lets him have one acre is a traitor to you all!"

"A steer needs grass as well as water. It's going to cost the Bar S a lot of money to keep moving their stuff. It won't put any fat on a yearling. And don't forget, they can't keep on driving cattle across your range. That's been threshed out in this county before. The shoe is pinching you now, but it will be the other way around before snow flies."

His logic swayed the majority of them. They effected an organization of a sort under Dan Crockett's leadership and agreed to act together. Even Quantrell consented to the arrangement. His apparent change of face did not fool Montana. He knew the man was dangerous.

The sun had set before they finished, but no one seemed in a hurry to leave. Jim was talking to Dan and old Lance Morrow when young Gene sounded a warning.

"Somebody comin'!" he called out.

Montana looked up to see four horsemen fording the creek. Once across, they rode up at a hard gallop. Hands strayed toward guns in the waiting crowd. The oncoming men were either part of the Bar S bunch or strangers, and with things as they stood, a stranger was more apt to be an enemy than a friend.

Montana shared the tenseness of the others. A moment later he recognized Reb Russell. Instinctively, the crowd had lined up to face the newcomers. Reb pulled his horse up sharply fifty yards from them and slid to the ground. Without a word to his men, he stalked across the intervening space, a mad fury on him.

Dan stepped out to face him.

"You've come far enough, Reb! I advise you to get back in your saddle and fan it out of here!"

A dozen guns were trained on him, but Reb came on until only ten yards separated them.

"You won't shoot while I'm facing yuh," he snarled. "You'll wait until I'm lookin' the other way for that." He saw Montana then. "So you're here, eh? I never thought you'd get down to herdin' with a bunch that would pot a man in the back."

Foolishly brave, he walked up and down the line, meeting them eye to eye with a sneer on his lips.

"Come on!" he burst out fiercely. "Which one of you potted that boy?"

The surprise his words occasioned caused the crowd to fall back. Men turned to their neighbors for an explanation. Dan and Montana exchanged an uneasy glance, sensing that the thing they had feared and hoped to avoid had already happened.

"Reb, I'll talk for our side," Dan announced. "I told you yesterday I didn't want any trouble. If it's come, I want to know about it. What's happened?"

Reb tried to glare a hole through him before he answered.

"Picked up one of our boys west of here at the forks

on Powder Creek about an hour ago. He was dead when we found him . . . Been shot in the back! Some skunk got him from the rimrocks!"

Montana groaned. "Who was it, Reb?"

"The kid."

"Billy?" Jim's voice betrayed his emotion.

"Yeah—Billy Sauls, your old buddy. You don't have to look so white about it. You're on the other side of the fence, ain't yuh?"

Montana let the taunt go unrebuked. For the moment he was speechless. The crowd was stunned, too, by the news that a Bar S man had been slain. All their deliberations had come to naught, for beyond doubt the boy had been killed by someone opposed to the Bar S. Being the sons and grandsons of feudists, they knew that only blood could atone for blood.

Old Lance questioned his sons. Dan tried to read the souls of his boys. Brothers looked at each other with suspicion.

"Hits natural to suppose somebody on our side done hit, said Lance, "but mebbe hit ain't so. Mebbe that boy had a personal quarrel with someone."

"I'll say he did!" Reb thundered. "With a hombre that filled four of our yearlin's full of lead from the same gun that killed him! You can't crawl out of it! One of your pack got him!"

"Men, listen to me!" It was Montana. He had jumped up on the wagon-box Dan had been repairing. His voice was charged with a deadly calmness that was more arresting than all of Reb's vituperation. "You know I'm an old Bar S man. I always found it a good outfit to work for; but I won't takes wages from a man who'll grind his neighbors under his heel and bring misery and poverty to women and children for no better reason than that he can make a few more dollars. All I said here this evening still goes. I'm with you to the finish. This killing hasn't changed that at all. But I don't believe you approve of shooting men in the back. God knows Billy Sauls never fought that way. I don't know who got him, but I aim to find out!"

"You needn't bother," Reb rasped scornfully. We'll take care of that! There's no need of any more palaverin'. Don't let me catch any of you above the North Fork after to-night!"

Without another word, he turned and stalked back to his horse. The light was failing fast. In a few seconds he and his men were only moving gray smudges bobbing over the sage.

"There'll be hell to pay now," old Lance muttered prophetically. "Talkin' won't do no good."

Montana was not listening. He was staring at Quantrell. The longer he started the more certain he became that the big fellow was aware of his scrutiny and was purposely avoiding his eyes.

"He's a tin-horn, and a tin-horn did this job." Montana could not put the thought away. Quantrell had been the last to arrive. His horse had looked winded.

From where he stood, Jim could see the animal.

Even now it looked weary, head drooping. The muzzle of a rifle peeped out of a saddle scabbard.

That rifle suddenly became of absorbing interest to Montana.

"I'm going to have a look at that gun before he pulls out of here," he promised himself. "If what I'm thinking is correct, it'll be dirty. He'd hardly have stopped to clean it."

Montana changed his position, moving about without apparent purpose, talking to this man and that, but gradually maneuvering so as to bring him nearer to Quantrell's horse. And now he was certain that Quantrell was watching him.

The big fellow had broken off his conversation with Brent Crockett. If Montana took a step toward the horse, so did Quantrell. It became a game.

"Well, if it's a showdown, let's get it over with," Jim muttered to himself. Throwing caution to the winds, he strode up to the horse. Quantrell was only a step behind him. It gave Jim time enough to insert the tip of his little finger into the rifle barrel. Quantrell caught him by the wrist as he started to bring his hand away.

"What in hell are you snoopin' around here for?" he snarled under his breath. His eyes were cold and fishy. "It ain't healthy to handle my stuff!"

"You might get a disease or something," Montana taunted. He was armed. His left hand had closed over his gun. "Folks are beginning to look this way. If you want an audience, you can get one in a hurry. Let go of that wrist or I'll do a little irrigating on you!"

Quantrell hung on, trying to save his face. He laughed unpleasantly then. "What's the idea? What are you tryin' to pin on me?" he demanded as he dropped Jim's hand.

"I guess you get my drift. You were the last to get here. You're rifle's dirty——"

"What of it? That gun ain't been out of the scabbard since yesterday mornin' when I killed a coyote. It's gettin' so you got your nose in everywhere—and you're wrong as usual. Why should I bump that kid off? He didn't mean anythin' to me."

"No?" Montana ground out between clenched jaws. "Let me tell you this, Clay—if I ever prove what I'm thinking I'll make that kid mean plenty to you. This happens to be something I aim to remember!"

CHAPTER VII

FLAMING SKIES

L ONG after the crowd had gone, Dan and Montana sat on the long bench beside the kitchen door. A candle flickered in the window of the log cabin beyond the barns that old Ben and Romero used as a bunk-house. A gust of wind shook the tall poplars in the yard. The stars gleemed frostily.

"Goin' to blow to-night," said Dan. "Cloudbank off to the northwest."

Jim nodded. Even in July, windstorms were not unusual in that altitude. His thoughts were of Billy Sauls, the boy who had been killed.

From the cabin came a snatch of song:

> "We rode the range together and had rode
>   it side by side;
> I loved him like a brother, I wept when
>   Utah died——"

It was old Ben, singing "Utah Carroll". His singing was lugubrious enough at any time, but to-night he seemed to hang onto every cracked note, as if loath to let them go. He was a lawless old Juniper to whom strife of any kind was welcome. His song drew a shiver from Montana.

"To shoot a man in the back and not give him a chance is nothing short of murder," he said.

"No two ways about that," Dan muttered glumly. "I guess it comes pretty hard to you, Jim. God knows it jest as well could have been Brent or Gene."

"You got any idea who did it, Dan?"

"No, I ain't!" He was speaking the truth. "It wasn't my boys, I know. It puts you in a mean place. A friend of yourn gits killed. Naturally you want to know who done it. But mebbe it'll be better if you never find out. It's war to the finish now, and a man's either for you or ag'in you. This boy was on the other side. I ain't approvin' of killin' of that sort; but it looks like one of our side must'a got him; least we'll be blamed for it. And right or wrong, we cain't go gunnin' for the party that's responsible. It's goin' to be taken as a defy from us—and Jim, we got to back it up!"

"I reckon we do," Montana had to agree. "You've stated the case exactly."

They fell silent for a while. Dan puffed his pipe thoughtfully. Gene and Brent came out and sat down with them. A subtle change had taken place in their attitude toward Montana. It was nothing less than that they felt themselves under suspicion. Unconsciously, Montana's manner was restrained, too.

"I don't like to say it," Dan declared gravely, "but it's a time for plain speakin'. Mebbe you feel you cain't go all the way with us now. We need you, Jim, but if you want to pull out—now's the time to do it."

"No, I'm staying," Montana answered with great deliberation. "I came into this fight because I thought you folks were getting a pretty raw deal. I reckon I'll see it through."

The boys had little to say. The tumbleweeds began to bounce across the yard before the rising wind.

"Gettin' dusty out here," Dan announced. He knocked the dottle from his pipe. "Might as well turn in, I guess."

Jim closed his eyes, but sleep would not come. He was too busily turning over in his mind what answer the Bar S would make to the tragedy on Powder Creek. He surmised that Reb was undoubtedly under orders to make a pretense of staying inside the law.

"But he'll strike back, and he'll hit hard," he told himself.

It was almost midnight when he sat up to find his watch. The wind was blowing a gale.

"Who's that?" Gene demanded fiercely.

"Just looking for my watch," Jim explained. "Can't get to sleep."

He paused to glance out the window. The sky was red to the north. A gasp of surprise was wrung from him.

"Gene, come here!" he whispered. "Look at that!"

"It's a fire, all right!" the boy cried. "Hey, Pap! Brent!"

Half a minute later the four of them rushed from the house, pulling on their clothes.

"It's Dave Morrow's place!" Brent exclaimed excitedly.

"No, it ain't the house," his father argued. "Too many sparks for that. It's Dave's hay! By God, it didn't take the devils long to strike back, did it?"

"And you thought they wouldn't do anythin' like that!"

It was young Gene. Jim sensed his hostility.

"Some of us better ride over there," he suggested. "It can't be two miles."

"You and Gene go," said Dan. "We'll keep a lookout here. I've only got about eighty tons of hay put up. I'll never be able to winter my stuff if I lose it!"

Scarcely a word passed between the boy and Jim as they rode. Each appeared to prefer his own thoughts. Montana had no reason to doubt that the fire was a Bar S reprisal. It thoroughly discredited his prediction, as Gene had already remarked.

When still some distance away from the blaze they saw it was Dave's hay. A number of others had come hurriedly. There was nothing anyone could do.

Most of those who had gathered there were young men or boys like Gene. Their talk was rife with threats of revenge and hatred.

The older heads had many opinions to offer about the route the raiders had taken, how many were in the party and what should be done in retaliation. Nobody bothered to ask Montana what he thought.

Dave, himself, tried to regard his loss philosophically.

"Better the hay than the house with half a dozen young-uns in it," he declared stoically. "I jest happen to be the first to git it, thet's all. They'll put the torch to more than mine."

"God a'mighty, man, you're right!" Joe Gault cried. "If they ain't another fire this minute over towards Jubal Stark's place I'm losin' the eyesight the Lord gave me! Turn yer back to the blaze and shield yer eyes!"

"And it ain't no hay this time!" Morrow shouted. "It's Jubal's house!"

An angry roar burst from the crowd. The burning hay was forgotten. Sanity had fled. In their present mood they would have torn old Slick-ear limb from limb.

Montana looked around for Gene. The boy had raced away already. In another minute all were raking their horses as they headed for the house on Powder Creek.

Furniture and bedding had been carried out by the time they arrived. Jim tried to organize a bucket brigade—the creek was near—but the high wind soon convinced him that the effort was useless. Indeed, they were fortunate to save the barn and corrals.

It was breaking day by the time the fire died down.

Quantrell had not put in an appearance, although the blaze could have been noticed from his place.

Jim said nothing, nor did he think it particularly strange. Things had come to a pass where every man was for himself. The thing he couldn't understand was the strategy of the raiders in setting a second fire deeper into the enemy's country after the first fire had been discovered.

"You'd think they would have run into someone with half the valley up," he mused.

And yet, their strategy seemed to have worked. Certainly they had made a clean get-away.

Dan was waiting for him when he returned to the Box C. Jim mentioned the matter to him.

"I'm going to catch an hour's sleep and then try to back track them," he said. "We got to know how they're coming down from the North Fork. We'll be ready for them when they come again."

By this arrangement, he left the ranch in the early morning and made his way over the rolling hills to Morrow's ranch. So many men had ridden over the ground during the night that it was impossible to pick up any sign that meant anything.

From there he shaped his course westward toward the smoking ruins on Powder Creek, keeping to the hills as a man might have done who was anxious to avoid being encountered. Once, where a spring drained away toward the creek, he found where a shod horse had crossed. The marks were fresh enough to have been made during the night. The horse had been walked across the wet ground.

"Certainly wasn't made by anyone rushing to the fire," Jim decided.

It was no effort for him to follow the trail to within a few hundred yards of the house.

The Starks had moved their belongings into the barn. Old Jubal was poking about the smoldering ruins. One or two others were there. Jim said nothing about the reason for his presence. Ten minutes later he headed west and crossed the Big Powder.

Once out of sight of the house, he crossed and re-crossed the creek many times, hoping to pick up the trail he had followed to Jubal's place.

He covered a mile without finding it. The creek began to climb toward the cañon. If anyone had gone up the Big Powder they must of necessity have passed through the gorge.

There, on the smooth sand, he found what he was looking for, but to his surprise, the tracks turned west instead of north toward the Bar S line as he expected.

He couldn't understand it.

"A man trying to get back to the North Fork wouldn't be heading west," he argued with himself. "First thing he knew he'd have the cañon of the Little Powder between him and where he was going."

Nevertheless, Montana followed the tracks, losing and finding them repeatedly as the trail climbed. Presently he was able to look down on Squaw Valley and trace the pattern of its many creeks. He could see the Big Powder, heading toward the hills to the north. Facing him was the black cañon through which the Little Powder flowed for over a mile. To the west he located Quantrell's ranch-house, and perched in the hills above it, the old Adelaide mine, the tailings a great yellow scar in the sage-brush.

There were no fences or marks to say where one man's ranch ended and another's began. Billy Sauls had been killed at the forks of the Big and Little Powder. Joe Gault claimed everything as far north as the cañon's rim. From that, Montana knew he was not yet on Quantrell's range.

"I'll follow these tracks wherever they take me," he thought, the conviction deepening in him that they were leading him either across the big fellow's range or to his house itself. "And one answer is as dumb as the other," he grumbled. "Quantrell wouldn't draw the line at burning a man out if he stood to make a dollar by it, if I got him figured out at all. But this doesn't make sense. And I can't believe Reb would send a man all these Godawful miles out of his way to get back to safety when he could cover him all the way up the Big Powder."

The climb became steeper. At last, he stood on the plateau that stretched away to the cañon rim. It was bare, save for a little dwarf sage. In fifty yards he lost the trail. Try as he would, he could not relocate it. The wind of the night before had scoured the high places clean.

"That stops me," he muttered reluctantly. "I might have figured something of the sort would happen."

The sun had climbed high. He got down from his saddle and squatted on his toes in the shade of his horse as he rolled a cigarette. A frown furrowed his brow as he smoked.

"Funny, losing the trail here within a mile of where Billy got washed out. Maybe it's a coincidence—and maybe it isn't."

He had left the Box C with the secret intention of visiting the spot where the boy had been killed, in the hope that he might find some clue. It was still his chief purpose, and when he had finished his cigarette, he turned north toward the forks, following the rimrocks. Three hundred feet below him, the Little Powder broke white over its boulder-strewn course.

It was impossible to get a horse down to the floor of the cañon from the side on which he found himself. Half an hour later he reached the forks. He was looking down on the tops of a grove of aspens. A green park showed among them.

"I guess that's where they got him," he thought. "Laid up here on the rimrocks and picked him off."

On hands and knees, he crawled back and forth, trying to find an empty shell or any other tell-tale sign that might aid him.

It was a futile search. Undaunted, he began the dangerous descent into the cañon. The dead yearlings lay where they had fallen. Beyond them he located the spot where the Bar S had found Billy's body. The tender sweet-grass and wild timothy had been beaten down by their horses.

It was no more than he had expected. Reb had been very positive that the bullet had sped to its mark from the rimrocks. The wound should have left no doubt about that. On the other hand, the bottom was so choked with brush and cover that a man could have crept to within forty yards of the little park without being discovered.

Montana was still pondering the question when he sensed that he was being watched. Someone was hiding in the aspens behind him.

He felt his blood thin. He was a fair target where he stood. Whoever was stalking him could not miss at that distance, even if he succeeded in throwing himself to the ground before the other fired. Wisdom whispered that it would be suicide to reach for his guns if someone had him covered.

He listened without seeming to. It was still again—ominously still. Suddenly his jaws locked and his body tensed. As though on springs, he leaped into the air and whirled. When he came down his guns were in his hands.

It came so unexpectedly that it caught the man in the

aspens off guard. Too late he tried to draw back behind a tree trunk. Montana caught the movement.

"Freeze or I'll bust you!" he cried. "Now stick 'em up and come out of there!"

The man raised his hands.

To Jim's amazement, Plenty Eagles, the Piute, stepped into view.

CHAPTER VIII

WHEN TRACKS SPELL FRIEND OR DEATH

MONTANA felt a little foolish. He had leaped to the conclusion that he had either walked into a Bar S trap or been followed by Quantrell. To find Plenty Eagles facing him was a distinct surprise. The Piute wasn't even armed. Jim told him to take his hands down.

"Where's your rifle?" Montana demanded.

Plenty Eagles jerked a thumb over his shoulder. "Back there with horse." He seemed harmless enough, even frightened. All of his belligerency of that day in Wild Horse was gone.

"How long have you been here?"

"Waiting here mebbe half hour—mebbe hour."

"Oh—! So you saw me come in, eh?"

Plenty Eagles nodded. Finding him there, it was perhaps only natural for Montana to wonder if he had had anything to do with rubbing out young Billy. There was a number of non-reservation Indians in that country. That their resentment over having their people removed from Squaw Valley had led them to take a hand in the strife was something he had not considered until now. If such was the case, they would be arrayed against both factions.

Jim thought, "It would have been just as easy for him to have crept up on Billy as he did on me. He could have set the fires, too. One man did it."

He began to question the Indian, but at the end of half an hour he was as much at sea as ever. Plenty Eagles insisted that he had had nothing to do with either the fires or the death of the boy. He claimed he had driven one of Quantrell's mule teams from Wild Horse north to Cisco and delivered it to the man who had purchased the freighting outfit. Cisco was situated on a branch line of the O. R. and N. that tapped the mining country around Iron Point in the Malheurs. In the old days, when the Adelaide mine had been a big producer, the owners had shipped their ore out via the Point and Cisco. Plenty Eagles said he had come in that way.

"What's your business here?" Montana hazarded.

Plenty Eagles became less tractable. "Not can say," he muttered. "Good friend of yours tell me say nothing."

"Yeah?" Jim queried sceptically. "Who?"

"Graham Rand."

"Oh!" Light was beginning to break on Montana. "Did he tell you my heart is good toward you and your father?"

"Say you my friend. Not thinking you send my

people away any more.   Not thinking your tongue is crooked."

It was said with simple dignity.

"I had a long talk with the marshal," Jim informed him. "The soldiers have gone now. Thunder Bird doesn't have to hide in the mine any longer."

The knowledge that Jim knew about his father won Plenty Eagles' complete confidence. "Can tell you now why am here," he said. "Bringing blankets and food for him. Buying them in Cisco."

Jim found it difficult not to believe him. He asked to see his horse and pack. Plenty Eagles led him up the Big Powder. The blankets were still wrapped in the paper used by the Golden Rule Store in Cisco. Inside the bundle was the dated cash sales tag. It was a perfect alibi. Plenty Eagles could not have been in the valley before daylight that morning.

"Your tongue is straight, *Cola,*" said Jim. "I greet you as a brother. But there is war here now. Men are quick to suspect one another. Some would even accuse you of the things they do themselves. If it comes to that, nobody will believe you. The thing for you to do is to take your father up into the high places. There is an old cabin below the Needles. He'll be safe up there. You know where I mean—above the mine?"

Plenty Eagles signed that he understood.

"Sometimes cold up there. So old man not hurting anybody," he argued.

It took some patience on Montana's part to convince

him of the wisdom of what he was suggesting. Thunder Bird had promised to meet the boy there that morning. It was past noon now.

"Nothing happening to him, eh?" Plenty Eagles asked.

"He doesn't know the soldiers have gone. I reckon he's afraid to leave the mine before evening." Montana turned things over in his mind for a moment. "Maybe I'd better ride up to the mine and get your father," he said then. "If you'll follow the creek through the gorge, you'll pick up my trail. Just stay with it until you get on top. I'll climb out of here and go on ahead. You wait for us above. Reckon you'll see us coming back about the time you get there."

With one or two exceptions, Plenty Eagles had no reason to regard his white brothers with anything other than hatred and suspicion. Jim's concern over his father touched him.

"All the time be thinking of this, Montana," he said. "Never forgetting, me."

It took Jim the better part of an hour to climb out of the cañon. In crossing Quantrell''s range he knew he was inviting trouble. It caused him no misgiving. After the Little Powder came out of the cañon he proposed keeping it between himself and the house until he was abreast the mine. If he ran into Quantrell or his men by chance, old Thunder Bird would be excuse enough for his presence there.

He was approximately half a mile above Quantrell's

house when he crossed the Little Powder. Cattle grazed on the hills, but he failed to catch sight of a human being. The country in general was swelling upward toward the Junipers to the west. The mine was located well up toward the head of a precipitous side cañon.

The old Adelaide had been a big producer for many years, until water had flooded the lower levels. No sign remained of the old camp, but the wood-road, over which tons of timber had been snaked down for shoring, was still serviceable. Montana turned into it and followed it around the hill.

Presently he was moving up the little side cañon. Someone, Quantrell possibly, had built a plank fence across it just below the mouth of the mine, evidently to keep cattle from straying into its several miles of tunnels and driftings.

He had almost reached the fence when he was surprised to see a little string of saddled horses standing in a pocket off to the right of the gate.

"That's queer," he thought. He looked again and recognized the horse Quantrell had ridden the previous evening. It caused him some uneasiness. "Got his whole bunch up here."

He couldn't understand what business they could have there, unless it in some way concerned the old Indian.

"Sure looks like I rode into a jackpot this time," he muttered warily. It was too late to turn back. He knew if he hadn't been seen already he would be before he could get out of sight.

Every sense alert, he slipped out of his saddle, and dropping his rein over his horse's head, walked up to the fence. It was head high. Through the spaces between the planks he could command a view of the entrance to the mine.

He had been watching only a minute or two when he caught the sound of voices. He thought he recognized Quantrell's surly drawl. A moment later, seven men stepped out of the mine. Quantrell was in the lead. He had old Thunder Bird by the shoulder and was hustling him along. Suddenly he gave the old Indian a shove that sent him headlong into the dust.

"Now clear out of here and don't come back!" Quantrell raged. To give emphasis to his command, he used his boot on the Indian.

It made Montana's fingers itch to let him have it. The odds were seven to one against him. And it was a hard-bitten crew that Quantrell had assembled. All were strangers to Montana, but by the look of them they were well-acquainted with the business end of a .45. Jim was fast himself.

"I don't figure to have a chance that way," he thought. "I'll have to talk myself out of this."

Thunder Bird dragged himself to his feet slowly. A trickle of blood stained his seamed cheek. Quantrell's foot went back to give him a kick that would hurry him up.

"Wait a minute, Clay!" Montana called out. "You'll scare him to death." His tone was bantering.

It was a startling interruption that made them reach for their guns. It was a moment before they located Jim.

"What's the idea?" Quantrell whipped out fiercely. "What business you got here?"

"Well, if you boys will put away your hardware," Jim laughed, "I'll climb over the fence and tell you. I got some news for you, Clay." He was thinking fast.

"All right, come on over," the big fellow grumbled suspiciously.

Jim perched himself on top of the fence and rolled a cigarette calmly.

"Let's have it!" Quantrell prompted.

"No rush, Clay. Kinda surprised me to find you up here whanging that old buck. I knew he was here . . . fact I came up to get him for Graham." The fiction had the desired effect on Quantrell. Jim saw indecision dawn in his eyes. Clay didn't want any trouble with Rand. He exchanged a furtive glance with his men.

"That's all right with me," he said. "The quicker you get him out of here the better I'll like it—and you can include yourself. Shorty caught him sneakin' down to the creek for water this mornin'. I got enough to worry about without havin' an Injun burnin' me out some night."

"Can't blame you for being careful," Montana declared soberly. "Some folks might find it handy to blame a fire on an Indian, but I guess we know where to look for the guilty parties, don't we?"

He was watching him closely. A puzzled look flitted across Quantrell's face.

"I don't know whether I get your drift or not," he drawled.

"I was referring to last night, Clay. Dave Morrow's hay was fired. A little later, Jubal Stark's house burned to the ground . . . Didn't you know?"

"Why, no! The goddam skunks! They ought to be lynched, burnin' a man out!" His surprise and indignation seemed genuine enough.

"I told you I figgered there wus a fire acrost the valley last night," said one of his men.

"I remember your sayin' it, Shorty," Quantrell recalled. "I didn't think it was any more than a little brush burnin'. . . . Can't be any doubt about who did it."

"It wouldn't seem so," Jim said without hesitation.

"Anythin' been done about it?"

"I was out all morning trying to pick up their trail. Didn't get anywhere to speak of. Reckon they came down over east and cut across the valley as far as the Big Powder and followed the creek north."

"That's about what they would do," Quantrell agreed hurriedly. Jim thought he caught a note of relief in his voice. "Makes all your talk sound kinda foolish, don't it?"

"Puts me on the end of a limb, all right. But I'm learning fast," Montana added cryptically.

Quantrell seemed to melt to good-will. "I thought you'd come to your senses," he said.

It was exactly the impression Montana wanted to leave. They talked about the fires for a minute or two.

"Guess I'll be going along," Jim said finally. He turned and spoke to Thunder Bird in sign language. The message he conveyed was unexpected, but the old Indian's answer was only a toneless grunt.

When Jim had climbed into his saddle, Thunder Bird got up behind him.

Quantrell swaggered over to where Jim sat staring at the valley below.

"Quite a view from here, Clay."

"Yeah! Lotta country down there."

Montana raised his hand to shield his eyes.

"You can see the place where the kid was killed, can't you?"

Quantrell was caught off guard. He craned his neck and stared with Jim. "Why, no—" He broke off suddenly. From the way his mouth tightened, Montana knew he had sensed danger. "Course all I know is what Reb said," he corrected himself. "I understood him to say it was right at the forks."

"I guess you're right at that," Jim murmured thoughtfully. He leaned over confidentially and lowered his voice to a whisper. "You don't suppose old Thunder Bird saw anything, eh?"

Quantrell repressed a start of alarm. Out of the corner of his eyes he flashed a glance at the old Indian. Thunder Bird's face was as expressionless as a piece of wrinkled parchment.

"Why, no; he's half blind," Quantrell muttered unpleasantly. "He couldn't see anythin'."

"He's old, of course," Jim nodded. "It was just a thought."

Quantrell rolled a cigarette with exasperating care.

"Still playin' around with the idea I got the kid?" he queried without looking up.

"Oh, I don't know." Jim's tone was guileless. "The news bowled me over last night. But it will keep. Reckon I threw the grit into you pretty hard."

"No hard feelin's; my hide's tough," Quantrell laughed. "Anytime you can pin anythin' like that on me—go to it."

That was Montana's intention, and their conversation had only intensified his suspicions. And yet, he managed a grim smile as he picked up his rein.

"So long Clay," he said.

"I'd go down with you," the big fellow volunteered, "if we wasn't goin' up in the hills lookin' for strays."

"All your boys, eh?" Jim queried, indicating the others.

"Yeah!"

"Looks like you're going in on a big scale."

Quantrell shot him a quick glance. Montana's eyes

were smiling, but in their depths he found a mocking light. It nettled him.

"I'm prepared for trouble—no matter where it comes," he announced. "I don't figger to take anybody's back water."

His men gathered about him as Montana rode away.

"Better make a bluff of combin' the hills until he's out of sight," Quantrell advised. "I thought he was goin' to be tough; but you heard the conversation. He won't make us any trouble."

"Don't kid yourself," Shorty grumbled. "I've seen his kind before; he ain't half as dumb as he pretends."

"No?" Quantrell dared. "Well, let him start somethin'. I'll take care of him in a hurry. No time to begin croakin' when we're gettin' all the breaks."

The others agreed with him.

"I ain't croakin'," Shorty argued. He ran his fingers over the red bristles that fringed his chin. "That guy's cagy—that's all. But what the hell! Both sides are at each other's throats right now. Whatever happens, they'll blame it on the other fellow. If this gent gets rubbed out—what of it?"

"Now you're talkin'," Quantrell exclaimed. "We can begin to get busy inside of a week. And we'll milk this thing dry. When we get through, if old Slick-ear wants to buy the place—at my price—okay! Let him put the money on the line."

CHAPTER IX

REPRISAL

MONTANA learned nothing from the old Indian. Plenty Eagles met them on the plateau. At Jim's urging, the boy harangued his father in Piute, but nothing came of it. If Thunder Bird knew anything, he was afraid to speak.

"I don't want you to mix it up with Quantrell over this," Jim warned the boy. "He's my meat. You go on up to the Needles now, and when you go out or come in again take the Iron Point road."

"Not got job," Plenty Eagles explained. "Mebbe staying up there two, three weeks."

Montana spoke to the boy at length and then turned his horse toward the valley. The sun was sinking by the time he reached the Big Powder. He followed the creek south for several miles.

Once he thought he was being followed. He drew up sharply and listened. It was only a coyote slipping through the brakes.

"Nerves getting jumpy," he smiled to himself as he turned east for the Skull and the Box C.

The day had developed little that was definite. If he was more suspicious than ever of Quantrell, it was a matter personal to him; and he decided to say nothing to Crockett. For the present he was content to play a lone hand.

The Box C looked so peaceful as he rode in that it was hard to believe that death stalked the range. The supper bell rang as he walked his horse into the yard. After they had eaten, they repaired to the bench outside the kitchen as usual. Nothing had happened in his absence.

"They'll get busy again to-night," Gene predicted. "Mebbe we'll git it this time."

"We'll be watchin'," his father assured him. "I ain't worried so much about bein' burned out down here as I am about the stuff we got on the range. Mebbe it'll look like backin' down," he went on soberly, "but I don't care. To-morrow we'll take the mowers and go down on the reservation. I'm goin' to cut my grass there and see if I can't make a crop of hay. Soon as we git it stacked, we'll move our cattle down there. It may keep us out of trouble."

His decision did not please his sons.

"What'll folks say?" Gene demanded angrily. "Mought as well let the Bar S have it all as do that! It's our range, Pap! Why should we pull our stuff off?"

"Dead steers ain't no use to no one," Dan replied. "I've got to have some beef to sell this fall."

By this arrangement, old Ben, rifle across his saddle bow, patrolled the Box C range on the south bank of the North Fork. The others toiled on the reservation for the better part of the week. Stock was being killed every night.

"We'll git it," Brent Crockett warned. "We ought to be out there day and night instead of stackin' hay."

"We'll be through to-morrow," his father reminded him. "If they'll jest hold off a mite longer we'll get our stuff moved."

That evening, just after supper, one of old Lance's boys rode in with the news that the Bar S had brought more men into the valley.

"Must be nigh onto forty of 'em here now," the boy said. "Ole Slick-ear is with 'em. They're fixin' up Eph Mellon's house."

It was unpleasant news. Inevitably it meant more strife.

"Where did you get your information?" Montana asked. "Were you scouting up there?"

"I had a good look around, all right," the youngster replied. He was not over sixteen. "Eph never should have sold out on us."

Montana was not concerned about that, nor was he surprised to learn that Mr. Stall was on the ground now. The thing that bowled him over was that boys as young as this were in the fray.

"Do you know you're apt to get killed scouting that country?" he asked. "It's a damned shame to see boys as young as you getting into this."

"Reckon I can take keer of myself," the lad replied. "I know how to use a rifle."

Before the boy left he got Gene and Brent aside. What passed between them Montana did not know. Later, the two brothers were aloof and uncommunicative. About midnight they stole out of the house. Jim heard them ride away. It was not the first time he had heard them leave late at night.

"They'll get over their heads," he thought. "Slaughtering Bar S cattle will grow pretty tame before long."

Although they did not return home until three the following morning, they were up again at dawn, ready for work. Ben came in while they were eating breakfast. The air was soon blue with his cursing.

"What is it?" Dan demanded sharply.

"That white-faced bull!" Ben boomed. "Deader 'an a mackerel! He was right on our own range, too! Somebody got him with a high-power from across the creek!"

"Oh, Lord!" Dan groaned as he fell back into his chair.

The white-faced bull was one of the few Herefords in that country at the time. Dan had paid a fancy price for him, in an effort to improve his herd.

The boys kicked their chairs out from under them and raged like two madmen. It was on Jim's tongue to tell them that if they killed Bar S cattle it was only natural to expect that their own would be killed in return. But he said nothing. He had made up his mind that if they wanted his advice they would have to ask for it.

The incident provided the Crocketts with a topic of conversation for the day that—as far as the boys were concerned—grew more bitter the longer they discussed it.

All hands toiled after sundown without finishing their task. Nevertheless, Dan said he would move his cattle down in the morning.

A great preoccupation rested on him. After the dishes were cleared away, he got out an old worn Bible. He read aloud as his wife washed her pots and pans. The boys had drawn off to the barn. Montana found himself quite alone.

" 'And the Lord shall deliver them——' "

It was Crockett, his voice solemn and sepulchral as he read on.

"Amen!" the boys' mother intoned reverently.

Jim fell to listening. Such religion as he had was born of the lonely places and the sun and the stars. Mrs. Crockett had finished her chores. He could see her shadow on the wall as she sat at the table with her husband, her thin frame weary with the toil and drudgery of a lifetime spent making a home in the wilderness.

Dan put the Book away at last and sat deep in thought. He broke his silence finally.

"The Book says to have faith and the Lord will help us," he said. "I reckon my faith will see me through, but there's times when it comes pretty hard. All our lives we been hardworkin'; we fetched the boys up to be God-fearin' men. Awhile back it looked like we mought have our reward and find a mite of comfort. Now all this trouble had to come ... It don't seem right fair to us, Mother."

" 'The Lord giveth and the Lord taketh away,' " she quoted. Nancy Crockett had first heard the words in a humble mountain cabin in the far-away Cumberlands of Kentucky. For her they had softened the futility of life and its bitter disappointments. "It's His will, Dan'el."

Montana was filled with a strange melancholy. They weren't young any longer. It was this or nothing; they'd never have another chance. It made what little he had done for them worthwhile.

He got up to walk down to the creek and back before going to bed. The evening was soft and balmy. He was halfway to the Skull when old Nell, the ranch dog, began to howl dismally. Ben must have come to the door of his cabin and shied a boot at her, for she stopped suddenly.

In the moodiness that gripped him, Montana found his thoughts straying to Letty Stall. The bitter struggle in which he was taking part proved how far removed she was from the environment that was his life.

"She'll never get the right of this," he thought, "nor understand what I'm trying to do." He could imagine the contempt in which Bar S men held him now. She would share that feeling. "You couldn't hardly ask her to feel any other way about it," he admitted.

It was well enough to say that she never bothered to think of him. That didn't end it. He knew her good opinion was the most precious thing in the world. There was some satisfaction in thinking he had never given her reason to suspect his love for her.

"I've often made a fool of myself," he muttered unhappily, "but at least I never was the presuming kind."

The boys were in bed when he got back to the house. Half an hour later he was sound asleep himself. It seemed but a short while, though it was really nearing midnight, when he felt a hand on his shoulder.

"Jim! Wake up!" It was Dan Crockett. "Where are the boys?"

Montana sat up, rubbing the sleep out of his eyes. "Why—what's wrong?" he asked.

"I'm worried, Jim. You know how they been talkin' all day. I don't want them packin' off into trouble. I didn't want to lose the bull, but I don't want them to git shot up over it."

"It isn't the first night they've ridden out," Montana felt justified in saying.

"What? Why didn't you tell me?"

"Well, I fancy they wouldn't relish my spying on them, for one thing. My talk doesn't seem to set well any more. I know old Lance's boy brought them some message this evening. I began to put two and two together right then. Sure as shooting, Dan, those boys have organized themselves into nightriders."

Dan ran his hand under the blankets of Gene's bed.

"Ain't been gone long," he said. "The bed's still warm." He stood up, his cheeks cavernous in the light of the candle. Montana saw him reach a decision. "Jim, I'm goin' out to git 'em," he announced. "Do you mind comin' along?"

"It'll be like looking for a tick on a sheep's back. Where are we going to find them?"

"If they're raidin' the Bar S, they'll go around by the head of North Fork, or try to cross it lower down." All the placidity Jim associated with Crockett was gone. The man's face was white and drawn. "You pull on your pants, Jim," he ran on. "I'll go up by the way of the Skull and swing over to the North Fork. You go around by the east. Mebbe we'll run into 'em. Whether we do or not, I'll meet up with you in the coulee below Lance's place."

Outside, old Nell began to howl again.

"My God, why's she a doin' that?" Dan cried. "You hurry up, Jim!"

He had their horses saddled by the time Montana reached the corral. Before he rode off he paused to repeat his instructions.

"And if you meet up with 'em, Jim, tell 'em I want 'em to home. It's an order from me!"

Montana found himself in an utterly ridiculous position. He knew the boys would not listen to him, should he find them. They had shown him all too plainly that they wanted nothing to do with him.

Once away from the Box C, he slowed his horse down to a walk. For one thing, he didn't share Dan's anxiety. The boys had been slipping out repeatedly. He had no reasons to believe that this night held any more danger for them than had the others. The route he was following was the shorter. It was his intention to time himself so that he would arrive at the coulee about the time Dan did.

The night was bright enough for him to see a long way. It also made him an easy mark for any lurking foe. However, he reached the head of the North Fork without difficulty. An hour later he entered the big coulee.

"Reckon we'll never get a flash of them," he thought. But five minutes had not passed before he pulled his horse up short. The night wind had brought him the murmur of voices.

"Somebody down there," he told himself. He slid from his saddle and went ahead on foot. He had not gone thirty yards when a gun was poked into his back.

"Stick 'em up!" one of his captors commanded. "Now walk ahead, and don't take yer hands down if ye don't want to git hurt!"

One of the others called out a warning to those down below. In a few moments Montana found himself in the grassy dell at the bottom of the coulee. Not less than twenty boys sat on their horses, waiting, guns drawn. A second glance revealed Clay Quantrell. The big fellow was urging his horse forward.

"Who you got there?" he asked gruffly.

"Jim Montana!" answered the boy who held his gun to Jim's back. Montana recognized him then. It was Joe Gault's son.

"Montana?" a dozen voices echoed. The angry muttering that followed told Jim how unwelcome he was. He saw Gene Crockett leap to the ground and rush at him.

"What are you doin' here—spyin' on us?" he whipped out, his face twisted with rage.

"I'll let your father answer that when he gets here," Jim replied. "I expect he'll be along directly."

"So you got Pap out tryin' to ride herd on us, too," Gene sneered. "Listenin' to you has done a lot of good, ain't it? Listenin' to you and your take-it-easy talk is makin' an ole woman out of him! It's about time you learned your place, Montana! We don't need you. We can pick our own leaders."

A wave of angry approval broke from the crowd.

"So I see," Jim said. His tone was chilling in its intensity. "The kind that doesn't draw the line at sending boys out to get killed but who take damned good care of their own hides."

"I take it you're referrin' to me," Quantrell threatened.

"You take it right!" Jim flung back. "This thing's bad enough without getting kids into it."

"Yeah?" Quantrell knew his audience was with him and he made the most of the moment. "The trouble with you, Montana, is you were a Bar S man once, and right down in your heart you're a Bar S man yet!"

By the way the boys received it, Jim knew it had been said before. The next moment young Gene proved to him how the thought had flowered.

"When you were in Wild Horse we thought you were our friend," the boy exclaimed. "In seemin' to side with us mebbe you was only pullin' the iron out of the fire fer old man Stall. How do we know you ain't with him lock, stock and barrel?"

Jim knew where he had got that. It was almost as though Quantrell were speaking. As he hesitated over his answer, a boy rode in to warn them that someone was coming.

"It'll be Pap," Brent Crockett told his brother. "We better git goin'."

"You're right, Brent. We got some work to do, and if it's any news to you, Montana, we're crossin' the creek and firin' their range. We don't aim to be stopped by you."

Finding Quantrell running things had made Jim change his mind about interfering. He decided that Gene and Brent should wait there with him. He told them as much.

"Better not try it," Gene warned. "We're fannin' it out of here in a hurry!"

Montana was not underestimating his danger. His smile meant nothing. His eyes were colder than ice. He had asked for cards, and he had to play them now.

"I'm sorry," he said. "The others can go if they want to, but you and Brent are staying here with me!" Before they could stop him, he had jerked out his guns. "Get going, the rest of you!" he barked, his eyes on Quantrell.

It was his undoing. Ira Gault was behind him. He raised his pistol and brought it down with force enough to fell Montana. Senses reeling, Jim heard their wild cry as they raced away, riding like demons.

They had scarcely crested the long hill to the north when Montana heard Dan calling him. What Jim had to say left Crockett speechless for a moment.

"The young fools!" he got out with an effort. "They must be crazy, Jim!"

He was for following them. Montana said no.

"You can't stop them now. The sensible thing to do is head for home." The back of his head was wet with blood. "Whoever fetched me that clip had his heart in it," he muttered. "You'll find my horse in the brush. If you'll get him, Dan, we'll start back."

They stopped at the creek and Montana bathed his head. His thoughts were bitter.

"I'd hate to have it said that a tin-horn ran me out," he declared, "but I'm almost minded to move along, Dan."

"I won't hear of it!" Crockett answered loyally. "I know you're with us heart and soul. I'll have this out with the boys, and with Quantrell, too, for the matter of that."

"Better not," Jim advised. "Quantrell's welcome to his opinion of me. I certainly have mine of him."

Dan refused to go to bed when they reached the ranch. Over toward the North Fork the sky was a dull red.

"I'll wait up for 'em," he said.

Long after Montana had thrown himself down on his blankets, head throbbing, he could hear him pacing back and forth across the yard, mumbling to himself.

CHAPTER X

THE HYPHEN FLASH OF DEATH

AN HOUR before dawn a cry aroused Montana. He pulled on his boots and stepped out. Brent Crockett was riding into the yard. The boy sat stiffly erect, his eyes stained with tragedy.

Two others were with him. They were talking, and their voices were charged with a grim determination.

"You couldn't do no good a-goin' back for him," Montana heard one of them say. The boy was addressing Brent. "Reckon we got to be men about this."

"Damn 'em," the other muttered. "They'll pay for it; we ain't done yit."

Dan held up his lantern, his hand shaking. The snatch of conversation that had come to them permitted but one conclusion.

"Jim—he's come back without Gene!" There was a sob in Crockett's throat.

"Yeah—" Montana answered tonelessly. "The fools," he added to himself.

It was only a moment or two before the three boys pulled up their mounts in front of the two men.

"Where's Gene? What's happened to him?" Dan demanded before Brent could slip out of his saddle.

106

Anxiety was written in every line of his weather-beaten face.

Jim saw a dry sob rack Brent. He hung his head and couldn't answer. The others seemed strangely reluctant to speak.

"Come on," Dan urged sharply, his voice thin and strained. "What is it, Brent?" The old man was suddenly a pathetic figure. Sight of him seemed completely to unnerve Brent. He broke down and began to cry.

"Pap—they got him," he sobbed. "I—I reckon Gene's dead." He couldn't go on for a moment or two. "Why couldn't it hev been me?" he moaned over and over.

The news shook his father. For seconds he stared dumbly at the boy and said nothing. Tragedy had been no stranger to him. He had schooled himself to its sudden blows, but now he trembled like a gnarled, timberline cedar that at last finds the blast too strong. His lips began to move, but he was only mumbling incoherently to himself.

Montana put a hand on his bowed shoulders.

"Come on, Dan," he murmured hopefully, "maybe the boy's only wounded. No use thinking otherwise until we know to the contrary."

He paused to glance at Brent. The boy refused to meet his eyes, now that his folly had ended so disastrously.

"I wanted to go back and git him," Brent muttered miserably. "The boys wouldn't let me do it."

"That's right," one of them spoke up. "Brent wanted to go bustin' back acrost the creek when he found Gene wa'n't with us. We had to cuff him around a little before he'd listen to reason. Wa'n't no sense in both of 'em gittin' it."

Montana turned to Brent.

"Brent—do you mind telling me just what happened?"

The boy raised his head reluctantly. Even now, crushed as he was, he could not face Montana without hostility. It surprised him not to find Jim's eyes accusing.

"We got acrost the creek, all right," he got out, breathing hard. "We set the grass afire right off, but it was dry and it flamed up 'fore we could git away." He shook his head at the memory. "Reckon they wuz aixpectin' us. They began to blaze away at us. Four or five of them cut Gene off. We heard 'em calling on him to throw up his hands. But Gene begin shootin' back. They got him directly. We seen him go down——"

"Then what happened?" Montana prompted. "If the grass was burning fast you must have been able to see a long way."

"They could see, too," Brent replied. "We had to git to cover or they'd have picked us all off. So we got back acrost the creek and waited—hoping he might show up. When he didn't come, I said I was agoin' back fer him. And I'd gone, too, if they hadn't piled into me that-a-way."

Montana had the picture.

"I guess it's just as well you didn't go," he said. "Who was running things?"

Brent misunderstood his thought.

"Ain't no use your blamin' Quantrell for this," he grumbled. "He didn't hev nuthin' to do with it."

"How come?"

"Why—his horse went lame," Brent explained. "Twisted an ankle or somethin' 'fore we first reached the creek. It slowed him up."

"Reckon it did." Montana's tone was bitter. "Pressed for time like that, I suppose he told you to go on."

"We couldn't wait for him," one of the other boys cut in. "We had to be back before daylight."

"Of course." Montana's tone was mocking. "I reckon Quantrell didn't arrive in time to go across with you at all."

"Why—no," Brent muttered unhappily, beginning to sense what was running through Jim's mind.

Montana's jaws clicked together ominously. He thought, "A Bar S bullet may have got Gene, but Quantrell is the real murderer." Aloud he said, "You know it's awfully easy to lame a horse, Brent—awfully convenient sometimes."

The three boys understood him, but they had no reply to make. Montana turned to Dan Crockett.

"Dan, I'm going up there," he said. "I can make it

before daylight. "Just keep on hoping for the best until I get back."

Crockett nodded glumly. Hope was dead in his heart.

"It'll be dangerous, Jim——"

"Don't think about that. Somebody's got to go." He spoke to Brent again, asking him where they had crossed the North Fork.

"At the monument rock. Guess you know where I mean." Jim nodded. "There's a big flat just above it. That's where all the shootin' wuz . . . If you're goin', Montana, I'll go with you."

"No, I'll go alone," Jim declared. He asked Dan to walk down to the corral with him. "Better keep your eye on Brent. Tell him to stay away from the house until I get back. For the present, Dan, I wouldn't say anything to the wife," he advised. "It may not be as bad as we think."

"I reckon it'll be bad enough," Dan muttered hope-lessly. "I seen this comin', Jim. I felt it all evenin' . . . Poor, foolish boy."

He helped Jim to saddle up.

"Don't seem that you should be the one to go," he said. "They'll mow you down quicker than any of us."

"Don't worry, Dan; I'll be all right."

He left without another word. It was his intention to be across the North Fork before dawn, and he did not spare his horse.

A breeze had sprung up. It was cool against his cheek. It helped him to think. Long before he reached the creek, he had decided on his course of action. In line with it, he crossed the North Fork a mile below the monument and headed for the hills so as to come out above the big flat where the fighting had occurred.

The rising wind alone would have told him that dawn was not far away. By the time he reached the head of the flat, the shadows were beginning to lighten to the east. Below him it still was night.

From where he stood it was possibly three-quarters of a mile to the creek.

"No use to go ahead on foot," he thought. "If I find him, I've got to get out in a hurry. I'll need a horse right quick."

The fire the boys had lighted had been put out, but the smell of burned grass filled his nostrils. It was very still. As he stopped every few feet, he could hear distinctly the purling of the creek.

The rolling plain was without cover of any sort. If Reb and his men were watching—and he had every reason to believe they were—they would locate him quickly enough as soon as it grew light.

"Maybe they don't know Gene is here," he mused. That would be in his favor. On the other hand, if they had found the boy, and he was not dead, they hardly would have left him there. Jim refused to believe Reb would be that heartless.

Minutes fled as he continued his search. The sky was already pink and yellow beyond the Malheurs.

He thought, "I'll have to be on my way in a minute or two."

He urged his horse ahead. They had gone only a few yards when the animal stopped. Montana peered through the purple mists and saw only what he took to be a low rock outcropping. He kneed his horse, but got no response.

"What is it, Paint?" he murmured. The horse's ears were stiff and erect. Jim slid to the ground. Three or four steps and he saw that the brown patch was a tarpaulin, not a rock. He lifted one end of it. Gene lay there. He was dead.

"Poor old Mother Crockett," Jim thought. "It's going to be awfully hard on her. He was her baby."

It took him several minutes to place the body across his saddle bow. He knew beyond doubt that the Bar S had someone watching the flat.

"Reb knows that come sunup we'd make some effort to find the boy," he told himself. "Ten to one I'll draw lead before I get across the creek."

The rock, known locally as the monument—it was a shaft of granite ten feet in diameter and at least forty feet high—loomed out of the shadows to his right. Montana moved toward it, leading his horse.

He reached it safely. The creek bottom was only ten to twelve feet below him.

"Better get across right away," he thought, "and take a chance on making it."

He edged around the rock and was about to pick his

way down to the bottom when he found four men stretched out on their rifles at his feet.

They were even more surprised than he. Two of them he recognized: Johnny Lefleur and Ike Sweet. Before they could throw their guns into position, he had them covered.

"Well, I'll be damned!" Johnny Lefleur exclaimed. "Where in all hell did you come from?"

"Just back away from your guns and start picking stars," Montana ordered. "You boys have got awfully careless since I used to know you."

He kicked their rifles off the ledge. A fifth gun rested against the rock. Five thirty-thirty's and only four men! He knew the fifth man could not be far away.

"Now you got anything else on you?" he asked.

Johnny had a forty-five in his holster. Jim tossed it after the rifles. He was about to speak when a movement behind him warned him, too late, that he had lost the play.

"I guess it's your turn to elevate," a voice rasped. Montana didn't have to turn to identify the other. It was Reb. He was almost as incensed at his own men as at Montana.

"Fine bunch," he sneered. "You'll live to a ripe old age, bein' careful that-a-way!"

"Aw, we heard him comin'," Johnny Lefleur protested. "We thought it would be you."

"Yeah?" Reb taunted. "You believe in Santa Claus, too, don't you?" The red-haired one took a step forward. Jim could feel something boring into his back. "You can drop that gun," Reb advised.

Montana obliged by flinging it into the creek bottom.

"I said to drop it!" Reb thundered. "What's the idea?" He told Johnny to slip down and recover their rifles.

His perturbation tended to confirm what Montana was thinking. His eyes were inscrutable in the cold light of dawn. Seemingly without purpose he shifted around on his feet so that he could catch Reb's reflection on the big silver concho that adorned the skirt of his saddle. It was like gazing into a convex mirror.

What he saw there made his blood run warm. Reb was not armed! He had stuck him up with nothing more formidable than his finger.

Montana repressed his start of satisfaction and stood with hands raised.

"The crowd you're trailin' with took an awful chance in sending you over here," Reb went on. "But I reckon men who'll send kids out to do their fightin' will stoop to most anythin'."

"If that was true, I'd feel as you do about it," Jim replied. "But I tried to stop those boys last night. So did that lad's father. They wouldn't have it that way. It takes a pretty raw deal to steam boys up so they'll ride out in the night willing to get killed to help their folks." Jim shook his head sadly as his eyes strayed to Gene's lifeless body. "But only seventeen, Reb—and wiped out like that!"

"Don't get teary about it!" Reb muttered. "I got two men on the way to Wild Horse with slugs in 'em. It's a long, rocky road, and the fact that a bunch of boys did the trick won't make it any easier for them. Now you can take that kid back where you found him. If they want him—let the bunch that came over here last night come and get him. I said stay out—and I meant stay out. Get goin', Montana!"

Jim did not offer to move. Johnny would be back with their rifles in a minute. He was not thinking of him. His eyes were fastened on the butt of a six-gun peeping out of Gene Crockett's holster. He knew he could draw it quickly enough. But what if it were empty?

He felt he had to take that chance. His manner did not betray the thoughts racing through his mind.

"I was taking him back to his folks," he murmured evenly. "I—I reckon I'm not changing my mind!"

His hand flashed out and closed over Gene's gun as he whirled on them.

"It's still my play," he droned. "Get over there with Ike—and move fast, Reb!"

Reb knew his man—and he stepped aside. In another minute Montana was in the saddle and riding across the flat, away from the rock. He heard Reb call to Johnny Lefleur. If Johnny had recovered his rifle he could pick him off at that distance.

Strangely enough, Montana crossed the creek, five hundred yards away, without a shot being fired.

Back at the rock, Reb was furious.

"Why didn't you pick him off?" he roared. "You had all the chance in the world!"

Johnny scratched his head reflectively.

"No," he muttered, "if a gent's got guts enough to ride in here and force a showdown like that on us, I ain't gonna send a slug into him just to ease my feelin's."

C H A P T E R   XI

WHERE THE DARK ANGEL WALKS

IT WAS well on toward seven o'clock when Montana sighted the little huddle of buildings that was the Box C. He rode slowly, Gene's lifeless body draped across his saddle bow. It was a beautiful blue and white morning, with the faintest of breezes stirring the sage. In the dazzling bright sunlight and clear, tonic air of early morning it was hard to believe that tragedy rode with him.

They would see him, long before he arrived, and know what to expect. He felt sorry enough for Dan and Brent, but it was of Mother Crockett, rather than them, that he was thinking. Gene was her baby and, in the way of mothers, her dreams and hopes had centered about him. Men break the wilderness and other men raise monuments to them, but it is the pioneer mother who bears the brunt of it. He knew it. His own mother had been no exception. Uncomplaining, she had moved down the Snake and on to Oregon, helping her husband to win a home on the range.

She had broken land with him, ridden after stock, with Jim in her arms, doing the work of a man as well as the drudgery of keeping a home together, applying

117

herself with such ingenuity as a man seldom achieves. Neighbors had been non-existent. When, by chance, they moved in, Sam Montana had invariably felt the urge to drift on to a newer country where the opportunities were greater.

For him it had held an avenue of escape. For his wife it had meant only moving on to even greater hardships. Through it all she had continued to smile, following him without question, but hugging to her heart the resolve that Jim's life should be easier than theirs.

"It isn't going to matter to her whether Gene was right or wrong," he thought. "He's gone, and she's going to find it hard to go on."

When they saw him coming, Brent and the boys got into their saddles and rode out to meet him. A glance confirmed the fact that Gene was dead. Although no more than they expected, the truth shook their surly defiance, and their faces were white as they turned their horses to ride back with Montana. Brent tried ineffectually to hide his emotion.

"They'll pay for this," he muttered. "We ain't done with 'em."

"Hardly the time for talk of that sort," Jim remonstrated. "You boys had no call to get mixed up in this—at least not yet. If you had listened to your father Gene would be alive."

"God a'mighty," Brent burst out, tears running down his cheeks, "yuh don't aixpect us to take ever'thin' they hand us, do yuh?"

"No, Brent, I don't expect you to like what they're dishing out to you," Montana answered patiently. "But you ought to be smart enough not to let them force your hand. Don't think you can win this fight by shooting it out. As long as Henry Stall can pay wages he can keep on throwing men against you until you're all wiped out. I don't believe in preaching after the trouble's done, but if you boys insist on getting into the fracas I advise you to follow a cooler head than Clay Quantrell. His fire-eating talk is a great brave-maker. It led you into a jack-pot last night, but Quantrell was damned careful to see that he didn't get a slug in his hide. Steaming up a lot of boys and then ducking out at the last minute don't set very well with me. I reckon he'll have a hard time explaining it to your mother."

It silenced Brent and his companions. They rode along with only the creaking of leather breaking the silence. Presently Montana caught sight of Dan Crockett, waiting at the barn.

"Better ride ahead and tell him, Brent," Jim said. "Ask him to get your mother out of the kitchen until we carry Gene inside."

Brent spurred ahead. Montana flashed a glance at the other boys. They were plainly desirous of leaving.

"Better stick it out," Montana advised. "It may cool you off a little."

Dan was waiting for them when they reached the house. He was a pitiful figure. Inside, Jim could hear Mother Crockett sobbing out her grief as Brent tried to console her. He got down and started to lift the boy's body down. Dan stopped him.

"I'll take him in, Jim," he got out with an effort. He couldn't keep back his tears as his hand touched the boy's face. "Gene—my boy—" he mumbled heartbreakingly.

"I better give you a hand, Dan," Montana insisted. "He's pretty heavy."

They carried Gene in and laid him on his bed. Jim pulled off the lad's boots and signalled for the boys to step outside. He wanted to comfort the father but he knew the folly of words at such a time.

"Ruther they'd taken the place—ever'thin' we've got than to have had this happen," Dan mumbled brokenly. "Comes pritty hard, Jim."

Montana nodded, afraid to trust his voice for the moment.

"I'll send word to the Gaults and Morrows by the boys," he said. "Mother will feel better for having some women folks around. You've got to bear up, Dan, for her sake now."

"I—I reckon you're right," Crockett replied dully. "Seems like trouble is the only thing that ever comes her way. I don't purtend to understand God's wisdom, but He has tried her sore." He raised his eyes to heaven and whispered a prayer.

"I'll just step out," Jim volunteered. "I know Mother would like to be alone with him. If there's anything I can do just call me."

Montana closed the door after him and spoke to the boys. They left at once and he went down to put his horse in the corral and feed it. For half an hour he busied himself doing Brent's chores. That indefinable air of sorrow and silence which seems to brood over a home to which death has come had settled on the ranch.

Even in the barn he could hear Mother Crockett's sobbing. Every time it reached him his gorge rose against Quantrell.

"There'll be a showdown some day," he promised himself, "and this is just something else I aim to remember."

Dan came out later. He seemed to have himself well in hand.

"Mother wants you to come in and get your breakfast, Jim," he said. "It's all ready."

"Now why did you let her do that?" Montana protested. "I could have made a little coffee."

"She wouldn't have it that-a-way. The batter was all made; so she fried some cakes for you. She's lying down now. Mrs. Gault ought to be here directly. She's a capable body to have around."

"Well, I'll go in if you insist," Jim offered, "but I'm not hungry."

"Mebbe you'd best make a meal of it, Jim," Crockett said. "I'm going to ask you to drive to Wild Horse. Be almost evenin' before you git there. Wouldn't think of askin' it of you after your bein' up half the night if it didn't seem as though you was one of the family."

"You don't have to say anything like that," Montana chided him. "I won't mind going at all."

"I knew you'd say that. Mother says she'd feel better if we had a minister to help lay Gene away. I think Reverend Gare would come if you can find him. He knows we can't pay much."

"I'll manage to locate him," Montana assured him. "I ought to be back here by the middle of the afternoon tomorrow."

"It'll mean pullin' out of Wild Horse long before daylight, Jim. I would appreciate it if you could git here by then. Brent and me will make the box. Mother wants Gene buried among the trees above the Skull. We'll find a pritty spot where he'll be comfortable."

Neighbors would dig the grave. Later they would carry the coffin on their shoulders to its final resting place. It was grim, even stark, but their very remoteness from those softening influences of civilization permitted no greater ceremony. It was seldom indeed that an ordained minister of the gospel was present to pray for the departed and solace the bereaved.

Dan sat at the table with Montana. He insisted on a detailed account of how Jim had found the boy. Montana told him, making light of his brush with the Bar S men. Crockett was strangely embittered.

"I don't blame them so much for what happened," he said. "All these boys know how to handle guns. You can't aixpect a man to stand up and let them throw lead at him without shootin' back. It's one life against another. The mistake was in ever lettin' 'em go. Just one man's responsible for this—and you know who he is as well as I do."

Montana got up and pushed his chair back.

"You bet I do, Dan," he said, "and some day I'm going to collect in full for it."

Together they hitched a team to a light rig. When Jim had filled a canvas water-bag and tied it to the end-gate, he was ready to leave.

"The grays will move right along for you," Dan informed him. "If you happen to think of it you might buy sunthin' for mother. One of them black shawls would be nice. Just ask Mr. Ruchter to charge it to me."

Montana followed the old reservation road. It took him south to the Malheur and then east by way of the Furnace Creek ranch. It required patience and a liberal amount of faith to believe that this ever-winding road would ultimately bring one to Wild Horse. In the rolling hills east of Furnace Creek it became a never-ending series of switchbacks. When one hill was ascended another rose before you. Beyond it were a hundred others. From the crests, it was possible to look back and locate the spot where you had been an hour gone. With all that country spread out around you, man suddenly became very unimportant, his worries and trials of no consequence.

True to Crockett's prediction the grays moved along without urging. They seemed to have sensed that their destination was Wild Horse, and they suited their gait and stamina to the length of their journey.

The day was not uncomfortably warm but by noon the dust-devils were dancing in the haze that lay over the hills and valleys. It was country with which Montana was thoroughly familiar, but as is uniformly the case with outdoor men, each new vista held something of interest to him. He had the road to himself, and the world, too, for that matter, seeing no one, save for a glimpse of a distant rider in the bad lands beyond Cow Creek Butte.

Only those who are familiar with that big country will easily understand his feeling of complete detachment and the sense of pleasant isolation that descended on him. He was able to review the events of the past few days with startling clearness. He had no cause to regret what he had done. On the other hand, he found little to encourage him. Men could best be judged by their past performances. Knowing Henry Stall as he did, he knew the Bar S would not give an inch. Gene's death would solidify the feeling against him below the North Fork. Undoubtedly it would lead to retaliation in kind. The best he could hope for was that the killing of Gene Crockett might so discredit Quantrell that the man would no longer be an important factor in the struggle.

"He'll be ready with a plausible excuse," he thought, "but people will get the right of this affair last night, and some of them will be suspicious of him."

In the late afternoon he caught his first glimpse of Wild Horse while still some miles from town. The road was down-hill now and the horses began to move faster. His coming attracted little attention. He drew up before the sheriff's office and tied the team. He looked inside for Rand and was disappointed to find him out. There seemed to be an unusual amount of excitement around the railroad corrals at the other end of the town. He was about to walk down when Graham Rand came out of the courthouse. Graham hailed him and they repaired to his little office.

"Well, we always put on a show for you, Jim," Rand said, jerking his head in the direction of the corrals. "What do you think of that?"

"I don't know. What have they got down there?"

"About three hundred head of wild horses. A bunch from Boise have been out rounding them up. They're putting 'em aboard the cars now. Some Belgian has a factory up there and is grinding 'em up for chicken meat."

"The skunks!" Montana muttered angrily. "Only a few wild things left and they've got to kill them off. I knew they were doing it over in Wyoming, but I didn't think they'd be over here rubbing it in our nose for a while yet."

"I figured you'd feel that way about it," Rand answered. "I guess it's profitable enough, with the hides and the oil; but it gets under my skin. We'd never have moved into this country or nailed it down for our own without horses. I figure we owe them a better deal than this. But that didn't bring you to town, Jim. Why are you here?"

"Dan Crockett's boy, Gene, was killed last night, Graham . . . You act as though you knew about it."

"Yeah. Reb sent a couple men over here all banged up. I got the news from them."

"That's right," Jim agreed. "Reb told me he had them on the way here."

Rand's eyebrows went up. "Reb?" he queried. "You been talking to him?"

Montana had to explain. The explanation involved Quantrell. Rand expressed his opinion.

"You want to remember this, Jim; Quantrell isn't interested in anyone but himself. He'd sell out his mother. I've known him longer than you. He's always been turning sharp corners. I knew he was grafting when he was freighting for the Government. When he pretends to get excited about looking out for other people's rights—watch him; he's got something else on his mind."

"That's exactly what I think," Montana agreed. "But it's pretty hard to lay back and wait for him to trip himself."

"You won't have to wait long," Rand declared. "He's always played an under-cover game, getting somebody to pull the chestnuts out of the fire for him. He's out in the open now, and he'll overplay his hand sure as you're born. He's a tin-horn, and I never knew one who didn't over-reach himself."

Montana rolled a cigarette deftly. A look of grim determination had settled on his face.

"There's no question in my mind but that he picked Billy off," he said stonily. "I aim to square that some day—and I'm not going to wait so long there'll be any chance of my forgetting. I don't know where this trouble is going to end, but I'm sticking to the finish."

Rand asked about old Thunder Bird, the Piute.

"He's hiding out near the Needles," Jim informed him. "Plenty Eagles is with him." He told Rand how he had met the young Indian and what had come of it. "For no reason at all," he added, "I haven't got over the idea that the old chief knows something about what happened to Billy."

"If he does, Jim, you'll have to wait him out; he won't tell you until he gets ready. I'd fix up a gunny sack full of grub for him if I thought you'd be going up that way before long."

"I been figuring on taking a *pasear* up there," Montana told him. "I'll just throw in with you on what the stuff costs. You get it, Graham, and toss it into the rig. I've got a little business to do for Dan. If you think the minister is home I'll go there first."

"You'll find him home. He's been out haying all week, but he came in this noon. Had a wedding over at the church. When you get through, come back here; we'll have supper together."

Montana knocked some of the dust off his clothes and was about to leave when a young man passed by. He nodded to the sheriff.

"There goes your successor, Jim," Rand explained with a sly smile. "He's an Easterner; name is Vickers. Not a bad boy, but he don't know anything about this country."

Montana tarried.

"What does he have to say?" he asked.

"Not much. He ain't the talking kind. But he dropped something the other day that I thought might interest you."

"Yeah?" Jim's eyes narrowed with apprehension as he gazed sharply at Rand. The sheriff's manner suddenly became serious. "What was it, Graham?"

"Well—he said the sale of the Reservation might be set aside."

Montana sat down again. "He said that, eh?" he queried. "What did he have on his mind?"

"I can't say, Jim. You know that Stall and Matlack stand pretty well with the U. S. Land Office. Old Slickear threatened to take the matter to Washington. I reckon that's what his attorneys have done. If he can have the sale set aside on the ground that you had no right to refuse his script, there's going to be hell to pay."

Montana did not answer at once. This news was thoroughly disquieting.

"You couldn't get anything else out of him?" he asked finally.

"No, he closed up quick enough; but you can tell when a man knows more than he'll say." He paused as he saw the effect of his words on Montana. "I wouldn't make too much of it, Jim," he went on. "There's nothing you can do about it."

"Except worry," Montana ground out. "My God, Graham, this is going to be terrible if it comes now. It would have been better to let Mr. Stall have the land in the first place. I know I was within my rights; but apparently that isn't enough if the other side has a political drag." He got up and took a turn about the little room. He stopped abruptly and faced Rand. "Do you suppose this fellow Vickers would talk to me?"

"You know better than that, Jim," the sheriff answered with some feeling. "You leave him to me; I'll see what I can do. If I get any news I'll manage to get it to you at once, even if I have to go over with it myself."

"Don't forget, Graham," Montana pleaded earnestly. "You know what this means to me. In the meantime, all I can do is sit tight. If a hint of this reaches Squaw Valley they'll follow Quantrell into anything."

That iron restraint which was so characteristic of Rand came to the surface now.

"You never were one to borrow trouble," he said casually. "I've known you to sit tight before without getting jumpy. No sense getting buck fever."

Montana knew his advice was well meant. It pulled him up.

"I'll allow anybody a little ague when he gets hold of a wild cat," he smiled. "When you're bucking the Bar S you're taking in a lot of territory." He gave his Stetson a jerk that brought it low over his eyes. "I'll get along now and be back as soon as I can."

He found the Reverend John Gare at home as Graham had predicted. He was a huge man with the horny hands of a rancher rather than a preacher of the gospel. He received Jim in his shirt sleeves and promptly consented to leave at three the following morning for Squaw Valley.

"You know Dan is pretty hard pressed for money," Jim informed him.

"Say, Montana, there's no price on my religion," the big man scolded. "The man or woman who wants it can have it for nothing or what they want to give. I've been putting my brand on the devil for a long while, and I've enjoyed every minute of it. As long as I can stack hay or get an honest day's work, I'm going to keep on trying to hog-tie that maverick. So you rest easy about paying me. If money was what I wanted I perhaps would be running a still somewheres. You can see what money and greed do. They killed this boy, didn't they?"

"I reckon that answers it in the end," Montana admitted. The Reverend Gare was no stranger to him. The man was a zealot, but there was no trace of cant about him. He was a tireless giant, and he threw himself into the task of saving souls with all the energy he used in the hayfield. His combat with the devil became almost a physical battle. When he spoke, a stranger would have been hard put to decide whether he was riding herd on sinners or cattle, for his language savoured more of the range than of the vineyard of the Lord.

He would not suffer Montana to leave until they had discussed the situation in Squaw Valley. Jim was surprised to find him so conversant with matters there. When he had finished, John Gare communed with himself for a few moments. He shook his great head gravely.

"I hardly know what word to bring those people," he said at last. " 'Vengeance is mine,' sayeth the Lord. They must not forget that; but I do not take it to mean that when a man is riding an outlaw he must sit in the saddle without using his spurs until the horse throws him. It would appear that they started in using the prod at the first buck; and I can't understand that, Montana. They are a patient people, slow to anger, even though they are the sons of feudists—and hard-thinking, too. I can understand Quantrell's influence, with his appeal to their prejudice and passion; but I cannot understand what his game is unless this is a three-cornered fight."

The statement was startling enough to arouse Jim's interest.

"I don't know whether I follow you or not," he declared.

"Well, you've seen two buzzards fighting over a dead rabbit, haven't you? While they're lambasting each other a third one flies off with the meat. Something like that may be happening now."

It planted an idea in Montana's mind that lingered long after he had finished his business in Wild Horse and was ensconced in his favorite chair in Rand's office. He mentioned it to Graham.

"It's only in line with what I said to you this afternoon," the sheriff replied. "What's his game? What's he after? Quantrell never was a fire-eater before. Now he suddenly blossoms out as a champion of other people's rights. You tell me why and I'll give you the answer to all this."

"I guess that's it in a nutshell," Jim was forced to agree. "I'm not foolish enough to think that under cover he is working for Mr. Stall. You couldn't make me believe that the old man would stoop to anything like that."

"Hardly. If Quantrell killed the kid he did it deliberately, not because Billy was trespassing. I'm fool enough to believe that he did it for the effect it would have. He knew the kid was popular among the Bar S crowd. They'd be sure to strike back no matter what the old man's orders were."

"But that was only making the fight certain," Montana argued. "Why should he have done that? How was he to win that way? His game was to hold on to what he had and try to avoid a showdown—unless he's playing both sides against each other."

"You've put a big if in it now, Jim," Rand exclaimed weightily.

"I don't know about that. I don't think it's such a big if after all. I'm beginning to see this better than I did before. Without being able to put my finger on the answer right now I'm convinced that John Gare was right; Quantrell is out for himself. As soon as the funeral is over I'm going up to the Needles and smoke the pipe with Plenty Eagles and the old man. If they know anything I'm going to get it out of them."

"It's worth trying," Rand yawned. He got to his feet and put his pipe away. "I suppose you're about ready to turn in. Three o'clock gets around in a hurry."

Jim glanced at his watch.

"Ten minutes to nine," he announced. "Time I was going to bed. Didn't have much sleep last night."

Rand locked the office and they started toward the hotel. A light in the court-house attracted Montana's attention. It came from the room he had occupied for over a year.

"Vickers is burning the midnight oil," he mused aloud. "I'd give a dollar to know what he's doing."

Rand laughed.

"I'll tell you, and it won't cost you a cent, Jim. He's writing to his girl. Does it every night. He's talking about bringing her out." They walked on without speaking for a moment.

"Funny you never got taken that way," Graham said without warning. "Always figured you would."

It gave Jim a start. But Graham had no reason to suspect his interest in Letty Stall.

"Just goes to show how mistaken a man can be," he retorted dryly.

"Don't it. Maybe you're gun shy——"

"Maybe I am," Montana drawled.

CHAPTER XII

HOME ON THE RANGE

NEEDLESS to say, the events of the night on the creek, which led to the killing of Gene Crockett, were viewed in quite another light above the North Fork. Reb, still smarting from coming off second best in his encounter with Jim Montana, had been summoned to the house to make a report. He sat facing the old man, twisting his hat and having a very unhappy time of it. He was fiercely loyal to his men; so if his tale was colored in their favor it was no more than was to have been expected. It left a lot to be desired, even to him, and he did not have to wait for Mr. Stall to speak to gather that he was greatly annoyed.

"This whole affair has turned out unfortunately for us," old Slick-ear stormed, slamming things about on his improvised desk. "I can't understand why you ever let them get across the creek, Mr. Russell. I've given you men enough to patrol it day and night. When we said *stay out* it should have meant stay out!" He blew his nose violently as if to give emphasis to his words.

Reb slid further down in his chair.

"I wanted to stay inside the law," he said. "We

couldn't open up on them until we caught them trespassing."

"You miss my point," the old man snapped. "I maintain that with a proper show of force they never would have crossed the creek. We said the North Fork was the deadline. They called our hand and proved we were only bluffing."

"I don't know about that," Red grumbled. "We made it pretty hot for 'em."

"They accomplished what they came over here to do," Mr. Stall retorted sharply. "I do not care about the range they destroyed; we can get along without it. It's the effect it's going to have that counts. They'll come again; they've got a double incentive now."

"You mean the boy, I suppose——"

"Certainly!"

Dull spots of color began to stain Reb's cheeks as his temper and righteous indignation loosened his tongue.

"It was the only thing we could do, Mr. Stall," he exclaimed with some heat. "We gave him better than an even break, but he wouldn't have it. I can't ask my men to stand up and take it just because it happens to be a boy who has pulled down on them and is blazing away."

"I've no fault to find with that," the old man acknowledged. "You were well within your rights. You know I am against bloodshed if it can be avoided. Ever since Sauls was killed I have been afraid some of the men would try to avenge his death. This affair last night hardly comes under that heading; but it will be taken that way by the other side. They'll forget that we had men wounded and be swayed by the fact that one of their crowd was killed. I'm squarely behind you on this point; you couldn't have done otherwise. But we'll pay for it. We're very likely to have a lot of stock killed the next few nights."

"I'll find a way to stop that," Reb muttered.

"I hope so. But remember this, Mr. Russell: I don't want a Bar S man south of the creek! We'll stick to our own. We can't lose if we outwit them. We've got the water they've got to have. That'll decide the issue eventually. We're here in Squaw Valley to stay . . . But now about Montana . . ." Reb began to squirm uncomfortably again. "How did you ever come to let him get the best of you like that?"

"I've told you what happened," Reb insisted. "The boys weren't caught napping. They heard Montana coming and thought it was me. It's pretty tough trying to stick up an armed man with your finger. I took a chance. I thought I was going to get away with it; but he called my bluff . . . I don't know what else I could have done."

"Neither do I," the old man snapped, "but the fact remains that he out-smarted you. It would have been better if you had taken the boy across the creek and left him where they would have found him."

"I was just carrying out your orders, Mr. Stall. You said we were to stay on our own range."

Old Slick-ear was thoroughly exasperated. He pushed his chair back and began to pace the floor, blowing out his cheeks as usual.

"You needn't throw my own words in my face," he raged. "When I give an order I expect you to use some discretion in carrying it out. I've had about as much of that man as I can stand."

"Yeah, I suppose he thinks he is somebody, now that he's got the laugh on us again."

Mr. Stall whirled on him furiously.

"Don't you make the mistake of underestimating him," he exclaimed, levelling a finger at Reb. "He's shown me enough in the last few weeks to make me wish I had never let him get away. I'd feel better if he wasn't in this fight. He'll be leading them before it's over—and he'll take a lot of licking."

Reb confined himself to a non-committal nod. The old man went back to his chair.

"Going to be a real pleasure to make him stub his toe," he said, more to himself than to Reb. He picked up a pen and reached for a sheet of paper. It was his way of saying the interview was over. His foreman started for the door. He had just reached it when two riders pulled up their horses in front of the porch.

"Who's that?" Mr. Stall demanded brusquely, Reb's surprise being quickly communicated to him.

"It's Miss Letty and Slim Wheeler from Willow Vista," Reb exclaimed.

"My daughter?" old Slick-ear exploded. "What's

that girl doing here? Mr. Tracey never should have let her come!"

"He'd couldn't help himself, Father," Letty answered for herself. She threw her arms about him and kissed him even though he tried to put her off. "When he saw that I would come, no matter what he said, he made Slim ride over with me. You don't act a bit happy about seeing me," she pouted. "You're cross as a bear."

He waited for Reb to withdraw.

"Who wouldn't be cross?" he grumbled. "It's no place for you, with all this trouble. I'm surprised you weren't stopped before you got here."

"We came through the Junipers—had no trouble at all," Letty smiled.

"I'm glad to hear it," her father fumed. "You can return that way."

"But I'm not going back," Letty informed him coolly. "I brought clothes enough along to last me for a week or two. I intend to stay here with you, Father."

She turned from him to an appraisal of the house.

"You're going to what?" old Slick-ear cried incredulously. "Oh, no you're not, Letty! This is one thing I'm going to have my way about. Squaw Valley is no place for you!"

"Of course it hardly comes up to Willow Vista," Letty trilled, purposely misunderstanding him. "But I see you've been making some improvements already. In time, and in the right hands, it will be a typical Bar S ranch some day—with hot and cold water promised. Right now it looks as though we're getting ready to film The Great Cattle War."

Old Slick-ear was purple. He banged on his desk for silence.

"See here, Letty!" he boomed, unmindful of Slim, waiting outside the door. "Will you stop this nonsense? You know I'm not referring to the conveniences here or the lack of them when I say Squaw Valley is no place for you. I mean it's too dangerous!"

"Dangerous?" she dared provokingly.

"That's the word! Lately you've been running over me roughshod. This time I put my foot down. I won't listen to your staying here. You're going back to Willow Vista as soon as you are rested—and that won't be later than tomorrow. Do you realize that we had a man killed just a few days ago. You'll remember him. He used to be at Willow Vista . . . . Billy Sauls was the man."

The news worked a startling change in Letty. Her father had no need to ask her to be serious now.

"Father—do you mean that, or are you only trying to frighten me?"

"I'd hardly jest about anything like that," he said, his tone milder. "Somebody picked him off, down at the forks."

Letty reached for a chair, her knees suddenly weak. She remembered Billy very well. For seconds she stared at her father, hardly knowing what to say.

"I—I don't suppose I should be surprised," she said at last. "I knew things must be getting pretty serious here when you drew on Willow Vista for reinforcements. Mr. Tracey said enough for me to gather that you were drawing in men from some of the other ranches, too. The place is an armed camp. . . . But about Billy Sauls . . . I remember him. He used to be Jim Montana's buddy."

"I don't know about that," her father grumbled. "It's enough that the boy was killed. And if you don't mind, Letty, I wish you'd quit rubbing Montana's name under my nose. I've had enough of him these last few hours."

Letty sat up stiffly, her lips whitening.

"What are you trying to say, Father?" she asked breathlessly.

"We had some trouble again last night. They came across the creek to fire our range. We had some men shot up. It was necessary to send them to Wild Horse. The other side lost a man . . . others may have been injured."

"But Montana—what did he have to do with it? It —it wasn't he who was killed?"

"Hardly—but he had a hand in it."

"Oh-h-h!" It was an exclamation of mingled surprise and relief. Until now she had not known that Jim was in the valley, taking an active part in the fight. She pressed her father for details.

"But I'm waiting for you to tell me what Jim Montana had to do with it," Letty urged.

"He came over later and—got the boy." It came as a very unpleasant admission.

"I should say that was nice of him," Letty declared with some feeling. Mr. Stall swallowed hard.

"Maybe you'd better speak to Mr. Russell about it," he muttered icily. "He can give you the details."

He got up and went to the door to speak to Slim.

"Better get the saddles off those horses," he said. "Tell Mr. Russell you're staying here tonight. You can bring Miss Letty's saddle-bags in."

Letty Stall had no intention of being packed back to Willow Vista. Tracey's efforts to dissuade her from coming had only served further to convince her that her father was in danger and that her place was at his side. She told him so as they sat at dinner.

Mr. Stall refused even to discuss the matter. Her presence had had a thoroughly disquieting effect on him. In his heart, he felt there was certain to be further bloodshed. He didn't want her that close to the conflict. There was another reservation in his mind, which he didn't care to go into.

"It won't do any good to discuss it," he said with great finality. "This is no place for you. It's dangerous, and it's apt to be unpleasant."

"But you insist that you are safe here," she replied doggedly. "If it's safe for you why won't it be safe for me?" She smiled faintly and waited until she caught his eye. "How sure are you, Father, that you are not afraid that my being here might cramp your style?"

"Hunh?" he grunted. She had caught him off guard and he realized it a second later. Even so he tried to cover up by pretending not to understand her.

"Come on, cards on the table!" she insisted. "I know you'll go a long way to win this fight. Sometimes I'm afraid you'll go too far. After all, Squaw Valley isn't so important; you can get along without it if you have to."

Old Slick-ear began to bristle instantly.

"I don't intend to get along without it," he rasped. "If you came here thinking you could talk me into pulling out, you're wasting your breath."

Letty had to laugh. He always ran so true to form.

"I agree with you that it would be a complete and utter waste of time," she replied with a toss of her head. "In fact, I'm not sure it isn't criminal libel even to suggest that I would harbor such a thought. You have said you will stay—and stay we shall, because the Bar S must never lose face. But we will fight fair— won't we, Father?"

"Fair?" he screeched. "I'll have you know that I'm the fairest man on earth! I never over-step my rights!"

"No, but you always seem to have so many rights— and you never fail to exercise them."

"Why shouldn't I? That's what I'm paying lawyers for."

Letty was his daughter and could be just as hard-headed as he.

"Lawyers will never settle this quarrel," she said when she had finished her coffee.

"No? . . . Don't you be too sure about that," her father replied mysteriously.

"Oh, they may win a decision for you—in court; but the real decision will be settled here. I'm proud of you; I don't want any man to take an unfair advantage of you. Whenever it's been a fight between men, or a battle of dollars and wits I've been with you all the way. This time it's a little different. I'm thinking of the women and children of those men and what's going to happen to them."

"You can't make me responsible for them," Mr. Stall answered with fresh indignation. "Don't accuse me of making war on women and children. I don't want to take anything away from them that belongs to them; and I'm not going to let their men folks take anything away from me that's mine. If you're trying to fasten the blame for this trouble on someone, put it on Jim Montana. But for his meddling, this thing could have been settled without a blow being struck!"

Now he was only echoing the stand he had taken from the first. Letty was hard put to hide her exasperation with him. What good to remind him again that but for Montana's intervention the Bar S would long since have taken possession of the entire valley and sent the little ranchers on their way with a pittance to reward them for their years of toil?

"If you still feel that way, Father," she said, "talk is idle. Without intending to do so you are really admitting that it is a fight to the finish now."

"I hope to tell you it is!" he exclaimed with finality. "That's why you're going back!"

"That's exactly why I'm staying," Letty corrected him. "When those men see how desperate the situation is for them, you can't tell what will happen. My being here may make a difference."

"I'd like to know how—other than to slow me up!"

"Maybe that's what I mean——"

Old Slick-ear gnashed his teeth. He wanted to shake her.

"It may slow them up, too," she went on. "I saw enough in Wild Horse to know that their feeling against you is personal. Someone shot at you in Harney Valley. I don't want that to happen again. Whenever you leave the house I'm going with you——"

"Oh, my foot!" he burst out furiously. "What sort of fool talk is this? A minute ago you were talking about fair play. Now you propose to have me hide behind your skirts. Well, I won't have any of it!" He banged his chair down on all fours as he got to his feet. "I don't know how you are going to amuse yourself while you're here. I don't want you riding away from the house, trying to poke your nose into trouble. You are to stay right here, where you are safe."

Letty tried to interrupt, but he scowled her down.

"My orders to the men will be to keep you in sight of the house. If you refuse to obey, they will bring you back by force if necessary."

Letty's eyes snapped. "That ought to be interesting," she said icily. She had never known him to be so obdurate. She dabbed at her eyes, hoping tears might melt him. "You—you seem to forget that you are my father—that I love you——"

It almost had the desired effect. She saw him pull at his mustache and knew he was wavering. The lapse was only momentary, for he thrust out his jaw determinedly and reached for his hat, ready to march out of the room.

"Your father," he muttered sarcastically. "Hunh! That's what I want to be; not your little boy!"

Left to her own devices, Letty found time hanging heavily on her hands. For want of something better to do she went to the kitchen and baked a cake for supper. Charlie Chin, the Chinese cook, looked on and said nothing. Later, from a comfortable chair on the front porch, she tried to interest herself in the activities of the ranch. A big freighting team pulled in toward evening with lumber for the new bunk-house. It created a diversion which drew most of the men in sight down to the spot where the building was to be erected. It apparently was of no interest to a man squatting on his toes in the shade beyond the porch. Letty could not recall ever having seen him before, and the scar on his face made it one to be remembered. Unconsciously she began to watch him, and at the end of half an hour she was convinced that the man was furtively watching her. Suddenly she understood.

"My bodyguard," she surmised, a frown puckering her forehead. Evidently her father had meant what he said. "He certainly didn't go in for looks when he picked his man," she thought. "No danger of me trying my wiles on this one."

Just to prove herself correct, she pulled on her hat and started across the ranch yard. Before she reached the corrals the man got to his feet and began moving in her direction.

"There you are!" she said to herself. "My man Friday, sure as shootin'!"

She caught a glimpse of Reb a few minutes later and beckoned him to her.

"Reb, do I have to thank you or Father for the faithful watchdog leaning on the corral gate?"

Reb pretended an utter innocence and half turned to see to whom she alluded. He saw Johnny Lefleur looking in his direction.

"Him?" he queried, with a stiff little jerk of his head.

"Yes, Handsome Dan," Letty murmured with chilling sarcasm. "What's his name?"

"Johnny Lefleur—" Reb seemed anxious to be on his way, fearing he was in for another heckling. "Your father said he wanted a reliable man."

"You did yourself proud, Reb," Letty teased. "I'll return him to you safe and sound——"

"But Miss Letty, you be careful now," Reb warned with great earnestness. "You don't know how serious things is——"

"If I don't it isn't because I haven't been told," she broke in saucily. "I bet you'd jump right now if I said boo!"

"If you'd been here last night you wouldn't have found it any joke," Reb sulked.

"Speaking of last night reminds me," said Letty. "Father told me about Jim Montana coming over at daylight to get that poor boy. He said you could give me the details——"

Reb ground his teeth together. "That's just his way of ribbing me," he groaned.

"Well, you seem as unhappy about it as he." Letty was not being facetious now. "It was a decent thing to do, and even though he is on the other side of this fight you might have the good grace to admit it. Just what happened, Reb?"

Mr. Russell had difficulty containing himself.

"You see, I'm pretty busy right now, ma'am," he got out nervously. "I really shouldn't be standing here talking away like this. It—it wasn't nothing much. He just—came over and got him."

It was such a lame answer as to leave Letty convinced that she had heard anything but the truth. But Reb was not staying for further questioning. He had hailed one of his men, and without waiting to excuse himself, had hurried away.

Letty returned to the porch to ponder the question that was troubling her. Instinctively, she sensed that Jim had put their noses out of joint, and she was determined to get to the bottom of it. But her surmises got her no where. She ended by deciding to put a question or two to her bodyguard in the hope that he might be able to throw some light on the matter.

In answer to her summons Johnny sat down gingerly on the edge of the porch and gave her a shy grin. In short order she had his name and the fact that, prior to signing on with the Bar S at Furnace Creek, he had worked for her father at Quinn River. Letty felt encouraged.

"Then you are acquainted with Jim Montana," she ventured almost absent-mindedly.

Johnny shied away as though he had stepped on a rattler.

"You—couldn't hardly call us strangers—after last night," he muttered sheepishly.

"Oh, last night, eh?" Letty echoed, her tone far less casual than she wanted it to be. "You must have been on the North Fork."

"Yeah, I was one of the reception committee," he admitted without enthusiasm. Letty took her cue from it.

"Evidently you were as glad to see him as the others."

Johnny's protruding Adam's apple slid up and down his throat as he gulped back his surprise.

"I—I didn't know anybody was makin' a holiday over it," he stammered. He was about to express a further opinion when a belated sense of caution made him pause, and he fastened his faded blue eyes on Letty. "Maybe your just givin' me a ride, ma'am," he said.

Letty quickly disabused his mind on that point. Within ten minutes she had a complete and graphic story of what happened. Her pride in Jim soared. It was easy to understand Reb Russell's perturbance and her father's irascibility now.

"I could have picked him off," Johnny concluded, "but as I told Reb, if a gent's got guts enough to force a thing like that down my throat I ain't agoin' to wash him out just to ease my injured feelin's."

Letty rewarded him with a smile.

"You'll do to take along, Johnny," she said, her eyes misting. She could appreciate the cool nerve and the danger Jim had run. Somehow it was no more than she had expected of him, and it warmed something in her. But having succeeded, he would go on to other undertakings perhaps even more hazardous.

She told herself she could not go back to Willow Vista—that she would not. And Johnny . . . she had him to thank for more than she dared put into words. There was nothing about him to suggest that he would burn chivalrous under pressure. But he had, and Letty could only accuse herself for having scoffed at him.

"It's just the old story again," she thought, "of not being able to tell what is in a package until you've unwrapped it."

She felt she had to be alone for a while. As she got up to enter the house she paused to say to Johnny:

"It takes a big man to be generous in a situation like that. I won't forget it."

Her praise bewildered Johnny. But he did not try to understand it.

"Reckon Reb doesn't aim to forget it either," he sighed lugubriously.

"Why, what has he done?" she asked.

Johnny found himself in a very embarrassing spot. He dug a boot heel into the ground.

"Not meanin' any offense to you, ma'am," he got out awkwardly, "but you know what he's got me doin'."

"Watching me, you mean," Letty nodded. "You—find it so unpleasant?"

"No, I don't mind it that way." Johnny found it easier to gaze at the distant blue of the Malheurs than meet her eyes. "As work goes it's easy enough. But——"

"But what, Johnny?" Despite herself, Letty was enjoying his discomfiture.

"Well, the fact is," he blurted out desperately, "I ain't never been called on to play nurse-maid before——"

"And the boys are rubbing it in," she finished for him, her eyes snapping with indignation. She could imagine what they were saying and it infuriated her, but she blamed her father, not the men. He had made her ridiculous.

"I suspect the harm has been done, Johnny," she told him, "but if it will make you feel any better I can guarantee you that your nurse-maiding is just about over. It will be as soon as Father comes to the house. I'm capable of looking out for myself."

"Gee, I wish you wouldn't say nothin'," Johnny pleaded. "I can stand it until tomorrow. You'll be going——"

"But I'm not going!" she corrected him. "I'm staying right here! The Bar S didn't use to be afraid of its shadow. But times have changed. We're fighting a man now who doesn't give a tinker's damn about the pomp and glory of Stall and Matlack, and everybody seems to be getting panicky . . . . well, you give my regards to Mr. Russell," she finished with killing sarcasm, "and tell him to be sure to have the men look under the bunks before they go to sleep. Maybe they'll be able to get a good night's rest."

Head up, she whirled angrily and marched into the house, slamming the door after her. It was a moment or two before Johnny Lefleur could find his tongue. He felt a little groggy.

"Jumpin' Jee-ru-sa-lem!" he burst out. "I'll tell him, ma'am—I'll sure tell him that!"

CHAPTER XIII

HER FATHER'S DAUGHTER

IN THE course of an hour, Letty found herself with a fine case of the jitters on hand, but she was still as far as ever from discovering anything that held promise of making her father change his mind about her staying. She told herself it was a situation calling for desperate measures, and she was resolved to stop at nothing to win her point. Usually she could wheedle him into anything she wanted. She knew she couldn't hope for success that way this time.

Without doubt she would be in some danger in remaining there; but not in any such measure as he insisted. It weighed lightly enough on her.

"It isn't as though I wanted to stay on for the thrill of it," she protested to herself. "He'll be more careful if I'm here—and my presence may restrain things a little."

There was a third and more potent reason why she was so determined to remain at Squaw Valley. If she refused to consider it now it was only because it frightened her a little to admit how much Jim Montana had come to mean to her.

Obviously it would do no good to feign sickness; her

father would have her packed out to a hospital at once. She considered other subterfuges, but they promised just as little.

"But I *will* stay," she insisted stubbornly, "and without being made ridiculous."

It was almost supper time when, from her window, she saw her father returning to the house. He had been up since daylight, but his step was brisk as he crossed the yard. There was something about the set of his shoulders and head that conveyed to her a sense of his power and indomitable will.

Letty smiled fondly to herself, for she was not only proud of him but in the last few minutes she had made up her mind as to what she was to do.

It was only a few minutes before Charlie Chin rang the get-ready-for-supper bell. On all Bar S ranches it carried a peremptory summons. Five minutes later a second bell rang: supper was on the table. The food was plain, but usually well cooked, and there was always enough for all. But there was no second table or provision made for late-comers. If you would eat, be there when the bell rang. If you had been out in the hills, rounding up strays, and chanced to return late, or were moving from one ranch to another and got in after things had been cleared away, you went to bed hungry. There was a time and a place for eating, as there was for everything else in the regimented world of Henry Stall, and his cooks carried out his orders with zeal.

Old Slick-ear and his foremen always ate with the men. Betty's presence never altered that; a place was made for her and she took pot luck with the men.

Having anticipated the bell, she was almost ready to go downstairs when the first one rang. She felt refreshed, having managed a bath and changed from riding breeches to a cool frock.

Her eyes were dancing as she regarded herself in her mirror. She was thinking of the men. They could have their laugh at her expense behind her back. Face to face they were helpless. It needed only a smile or the simplest attention to confound them utterly. So if she lingered over her toilette tonight it was with malice aforethought.

Her father called to her as she was examining her mouth critically.

"I'll be down right away," she called back. But she did not go at once because she had caught sight of two men riding into the yard. They were gray with dust, and she knew they had come a long way. One of them she recognized as Tiny Melody, a Bar S man of long standing. He had a leather pouch hung over his saddle bow. From it she gathered that he was bringing in the mail from Vale.

It was the other man, rather than Tiny, who interested her. She found him strangely familiar, and before he had dismounted recognized in him Seth MacMasters from San Francisco, one of her father's attorneys. That he had journeyed so far from home and made the long ride in from Vale hinted that his business there must be of the most urgent nature.

Not only was her curiosity instantly aroused but she was conscious of a feeling of alarm. Surmising that she would get no information from her father concerning the secret mission which had brought MacMasters there, she hurried downstairs, hoping to overhear enough to give her some hint of what had brought him.

She heard her father's exclamation of surprise as MacMasters entered. Certainly he had not expected him.

"I had expected a letter, or even a wire," he said, "but to see you in person, Mr. MacMasters——"

"It's been an experience, coming here," the lawyer laughed heartily. "I never thought I'd be able to get out of that saddle unless you got me a derrick; but when your man, Melody, heard the bell and began to put on the pressure, I found I was hungrier than I was sore. I hope I'm here in time."

"Just in time. . . . Nothing wrong?"

"Quite the contrary," MacMasters beamed. "I'll need you in Vale tomorrow afternoon. Judge Robbins will wait for us. I have some things to discuss that I didn't want to put on paper."

Old Slick-ear thought he understood him now.

"Then you've heard from——"

"Yes, and very promising news," his lawyer broke in. He had caught a glimpse of Letty Stall on the stairs. He turned to her with outstretched hand. "This is a surprise all around, I think," he smiled. "I hardly expected to find you here, Letty."

"I only arrived today," she told him, "and I'm leaving tomorrow. Father insists on it, and I daresay he's right." She had overheard every word they had spoken, but she was as much at sea as ever. Although she was addressing herself to MacMasters she managed a furtive glance at her father. He was having a hard time hiding his surprise over her apparent change of mind.

"Undoubtedly he is right," MacMasters said. He had caught Letty's glance at her father, and knowing them so well, was not fooled by either. "It can't be particularly pleasant for you here right now. The girls have gone down to Carmel for the summer. Why not join them for a few weeks?" His daughters were Letty's age, and they were fond of one another.

"Sounds promising," she smiled innocently. "I had thought of going back to Willow Vista, but you are making me change my mind. If Father thought it safe for me to go out to the railroad I believe I'd go."

Old Slick-ear jumped at the chance she was offering him. He wanted nothing better than to have her back in California.

"I wouldn't want you to go out by the way of Wild Horse," he said, "but we'll be going to Vale early in the morning. You could go with us, Letty."

She hesitated, as though rolling the matter over in her mind. It was quite convincing.

"Well—I think I'll go with you," she said finally. "You can have Mr. Tracey send my trunk down from Willow Vista."

"Don't worry about that," her father exclaimed brusquely. "That will be taken care of." He turned to MacMasters. "If you want to knock a little of the dust off you and wash up we'd better get at it. You can step into my room."

Knowing the routine of the Bar S ranches as well as anyone, he spent only a minute or two in refreshing himself. When he rejoined them he offered Letty his arm and they went into the dining-room.

Instantly all eyes fell. Mr. Stall sat down at the head of the table, with his foreman at his left and Letty to his right. MacMasters found a place next to Reb. The attorney remembered Reb and shook hands with him. The men had suddenly become tongue-tied. Letty's presence alone would have embarrassed them to silence. She and MacMasters together—they had learned about him from Tiny—were just too much for them.

It was strange what a serious business they could make of eating. The food was on platters. Some of it had to pass a long way. A man would look up and say, "Pass the bread." Instantly his eyes would return to his plate. The bread would start moving, and eventually he would help himself to it. No one bothered to say please. Possibly because when they said, "Pass the bread," or "Pass the beans," it was a command, not a request. They were stark sounds, rising above the clatter of knives and forks.

Mr. Stall and MacMasters had very little to say themselves, and that little concerned such casual things as the market and the political situation. Letty lost interest in them and applied herself to her promised revenge. It was not difficult for her to surmise which of the men had started the laugh at Johnny Lefleur's expense. Ike Sweet, who had been with Johnny on the North Fork, and Kin Lamb were undoubtedly the guilty ones. They were seated within striking distance. Letty singled out old Ike.

He seemed to feel her eyes on him. She could see his neck redden.

"Please pass the hors d'oeuvres," she asked him.

Ike stiffened, but he did not look up. He knew she was speaking to him. The men on either side of him only ate more rapidly. Letty repeated her request and continued to stare at Ike until he had to look up, a look of dumb wonder on his face.

"I'm sorry," she smiled sweetly. "The pickles, please——"

In his anxiety to get them to her swiftly, Ike almost upset them. Mr. Stall and MacMasters missed this byplay. The others were keenly aware of it, for all that they ate on with stony faces. Indeed, this was something that was destined to follow Ike for some years to come.

Kin Lamb, across the table from Ike, was enjoying

it to the full behind his sullen mask until Letty suddenly turned on him and began to bombard him with requests to pass one thing after another to her until her plate was piled high with more food than she could have consumed in several days. With any effort on her part she could have reached out and taken the dishes he offered, and he would not have had to extend himself. But that was not part of her plan. She made him half arise, and then thanked him so fulsomely that after a few minutes he gulped down a cup of coffee and bolted from the room. Some one tittered. It was Johnny Lefleur. Letty gave him a knowing wink. It so emboldened him that he looked Ike in the eye and said, "Pass them *ore-dough* pickles."

Ike could have killed him with pleasure. Letty suspected as much and enjoyed it accordingly.

Supper was no sooner over than Reb began dispatching his men to the front, spreading them out along the North Fork and west of the Big Powder, north of Quantrell's line.

While her father was conferring with Reb and acquainting him with the fact that he was leaving for Vale in the morning, to be gone at least forty-eight hours, Letty sat on the porch with MacMasters.

It was a witching hour, the whippoorwills calling plaintively as they sailed over the sage. The Malheurs and the Juniper Hills were deep purple blurs. The valley itself was majestically beautiful in the mauve and lavender afterglow.

With all the cunning she could command, Letty tried valiantly to draw from the lawyer the reason for his presence. She failed dismally, MacMasters turning her queries with ease born of long professional experience.

When old Slick-ear came in, he bundled her off to her room with scant ceremony. He was anxious to hear what MacMasters had to say.

They talked for a long time. It was after nine when Letty heard them saying good-night. Her light was out, but she was not asleep. From her window she had a distant view of the North Fork. The moon had risen and the night was so bright that she could see an incredible distance.

She found her thoughts turning to Jim Montana. He was sound asleep in Wild Horse at the moment. She didn't know that; and not knowing, she thought only of the danger he might be in. MacMasters' sudden appearance was linked in her mind with the mysterious remark her father had made that day anent the courts still having something to say about this struggle. Whatever the move was, it was evidently coming to a head even sooner than her father had figured. That it could portend anything but ill for the other side seemed a foregone conclusion.

It distressed her to have to admit that her sympathies were not with her father. It savoured of disloyalty, and she reproached herself bitterly. But that did not alter the case.

"I can't help feeling they are the underdog in this,"

she thought. "The Bar S is rich and powerful; they're poor and helpless, in a way. Doesn't seem to be the sporting thing to crush them."

She and Montana viewed the struggle in quite the same light, yet it did not occur to her that his championing of their cause had influenced her at all.

"There are rights involved here which the law may not recognize," she mused on; "but they are rights, just the same. Jim recognized that. I wish I could do something to help him."

The night was very still. Several times she listened carefully, but the vagrant breeze brought no sound of strife to her ears. It was nearing midnight before she closed her eyes and slept, a prayer for Jim's safety on her lips.

Her father rapped on her door at half past five. At six o'clock they were having breakfast. Reb came in. The night had passed without a shot being fired.

"Don't take anything for granted while I'm gone," the old man warned him. "I'll be surprised if you don't hear from them before I get back."

In a few minutes they were ready to leave. Vale lay beyond the Malheurs, to the northeast. There was no road. The trail they followed had been used for years. Over it the corral poles and fence posts used on the ranch had been snaked down from the foothills.

At first they rode abreast. The air was keen and bracing, MacMasters found the scene inspiriting. Old Slick-ear was in a congenial mood. Letty seemed in the best of spirits, keeping up a running fire of conversation with them as opportunity permitted.

In the course of an hour the buck brush and clumps of willow along the dry wash of what in early spring was a flowing creek, leading to the Big Powder, began to bar the way. They strung out in single file, and Letty managed it so she drew up in the rear. For seconds at a time they were out of sight of one another.

Not more than fifteen minutes had passed when Mr. Stall and MacMasters heard Letty scream. They looked back to see her horse rearing and plunging back over the trail they had just come.

They wheeled their horses at once and took after her. Screened by the willows, she pulled her pony up, dropped the reins over his head and flung herself on the ground.

It was only a minute before they found her. Her eyes were closed and she was groaning piteously. Her father leaped out of his saddle and cradled her head in his arms. If she could have seen his concern she undoubtedly would not have had the courage to carry through her deception.

"Letty—" he called. "Are you hurt?"

"I guess she's fainted," she heard MacMasters say. The two men were bending over her.

Letty opened her eyes slowly, a look of pretended pain twisting her lips. Her father was somewhat relieved. He asked MacMasters to get his canteen. He held it to her lips and made her sip a little water.

"What happened?" he demanded anxiously.

"My horse almost stepped on a rattler," she lied convincingly. "I—I wasn't ready for it." Her voice sounded very weak and faint.

"Well, are you hurt?"

"My ankle—" she groaned. "It's driving me mad. I—I'm afraid you'll have to cut my boot."

Mr. Stall soon had the boot cut away so it could be removed. Letty obliged with a heart-rending groan as it came off.

"It doesn't look swollen," her father said when he had removed her stocking.

"It'll begin to swell in a few minutes," MacMasters put in, having been completely deceived. "You were lucky not to get a broken leg. We ought to bind it up right away."

Letty told them there was a skirt in her saddle bag that would serve the purpose. They got it at once and tore it into strips.

"Not so tight, Father!" she protested as old Slick-ear bound the ankle. "Are you sure it isn't broken?"

"Why, no," he grumbled. "It's just a little sprain." He had begun to realize what a predicament he was in. Obviously Letty could not go on to Vale with them. He would have to take her back to the ranch and leave her there. He turned to his attorney. "This complicates things for us, Mr. MacMasters," he said. "It doesn't look as though we could possibly get to Vale before evening now. We are going to lose two or three hours at best. We'll have to return to the ranch."

"Naturally," MacMasters said with good grace. "We can save a few minutes if we get started at once." He turned to address Letty. "Do you think you can stay in your saddle if we lift you up? We'll walk the horses."

"I'll take her up with me," her father suggested. "It'll be easier on her and we can make better time." He chewed at his mustache as usual when greatly perturbed. "I didn't want you to stay at the ranch," he told her, "but it looks as though there was nothing else to do now."

Letty gazed up at him with well-stimulated agony.

"Father—I don't want to stay at the ranch," she sighed. "If you could get a rig we could drive out——"

"We'd have to go all the way around by Iron Point," he cut her off. "It isn't to be thought of. I'm due in Vale this afternoon. Yesterday you insisted on staying; now you won't have it." He shook his head hopelessly. "I can't understand you at all. If you have to stay at the ranch, you can do it, can't you? It isn't so bad as that."

"But there's nothing to do. I thought it would be exciting. And the men—they're all laughing at me behind my back."

"What?" he exploded. "Laughing over what?"

"Over my chaperon. . . . As though I were a child! I heard what they were saying. Calling him my nurse-maid! I won't stand it, Father! I refuse to stay there!"

"Now see here, Letty," he grumbled, "no sense making a mountain out of a mole hill. If you have to stay there for a few days you will. I've got a right to expect some co-operation from you. As for having a man to watch you—I did it only because I was afraid you'd get adventurous and run into trouble. You'll not be able to do much running about now; so I'll put you on your own. I'll send a note to Mr. Russell."

Letty gave in grudgingly. When she finally said yes he gave her hand a little pat of affection.

"I'll bring you an armful of books and magazines," he promised. "It may be some days before you'll be able to leave."

Their return to the ranch was of necessity slow. They had returned to within two miles of the house when old Slick-ear saw one of his men, off to the east. He hailed him.

"If you could go in with him," he suggested to Letty, "we could save an hour. You'll find some liniment and arnica in my room. You'll be able to do about as much for yourself as I could."

Letty propped herself up to get a glimpse of the oncoming rider. She was delighted to discover that it was Kin Lamb.

"I've made you trouble enough, Father," she sighed. "There's no need of making you go all the way back to the house."

Kin's face fell when he learned that he was to carry

Letty back to the ranch. But an order was an order.

They transferred her to his horse, and Letty took a death grip on him. Her father warned him to be careful of her.

"Yes, sir," Kin muttered. The "sir" in itself was proof enough of his agony.

They parted a few minutes later and soon lost sight of one another. Letty heaved a sigh of relief. She had won hands down, and her cup was still brimming over. She tightened her hold on Kin and pillowed her head on his shoulder.

"Maybe I best leave you here and fetch a rig if you're feelin' so bad," he suggested desperately. In a quarter of an hour they would be approaching the house. He dreaded being seen with Letty Stall draped over him, her arms about his neck.

"It'll be better if we don't stop," Letty insisted. "I— I'm not tiring you, Kin?"

"Oh, no—not at all," he drawled unhappily. His face was beet red.

"I'll feel better when I get to the house——"

"So will I," he thought. The boys would be working on the new bunk-house. They'd all be there to observe him.

Letty knew what was running through his mind. As they drew nearer the yard she snuggled even closer to him.

"I'm afraid I'm a terrible nuisance," she purred. "Making nurse-maids of all of you——"

The barb that lay in her words sunk into Kin's consciousness with a savage plunge.

The reception that awaited them measured up fully to Kin's worst expectations. In a dead silence they rode past the new bunk-house, and Kin looked neither to right nor left.

Reb appeared just as they reached the house. He carried Letty inside.

"Maybe I'd ought to carry you up to your room," he suggested.

"No, I can limp up all right," Letty smiled. "You might get the arnica for me from Father's room."

Reb obliged. Letty took it, and handing him the note her father had sent, began to limp up the stairs, leaning heavily on the railing.

Reb had finished reading Mr. Stall's note and was regarding her with growing amazement. Letty was limping perfectly, but she was favoring the wrong foot. Light began to break on Reb as his nimble brain pondered the fact.

"You'll be stayin' then, I guess," he said stonily.

"For a while," Letty answered without looking back.

"I thought so," Reb muttered knowingly to himself.

CHAPTER XIV

"VENGEANCE IS MINE!"

A FAINT breeze stirred the aspens to murmurous lamentation as the Reverend John Gare stood at the head of the freshly made grave on the hillside above the Skull and consigned all that was mortal of Gene Crockett to the dust of his fathers.

The house had proven far too small to accommodate the crowd that had come for the funeral. At Gare's suggestion they had held the services in the yard, under the big cottonwood. He had spoken at length, interlarding the sonorous phrases of the Bible with the homely wisdom of one who knew how to reach their hearts.

He did not torture Mother Crockett and Dan by attempting to eulogize the boy. He spoke of God's mercy; of the strange ways in which He brings his miracles to pass.

A blanket had been thrown over the rough pine box which Dan and Brent had built for Gene. Gare stood beside it, the black-bonneted women and sober-faced men ringed about him in a half circle. His frock coat, long since faded to a dull bottle green, his shaggy hair and unbuttoned shirt did not detract from the magnetism of the man. He had brought the Word to them, and they listened with bowed heads.

Mother Crockett, tearless now, hung on his words. Gene was having a Christian burial, and it fortified her. Dan stood on one side of her, Brent on the other, clasping her hands.

Montana told himself he would never forget that picture. He was humble in the face of their fortitude. It was that very quality which had first won him to them. From within themselves, they had drawn strength with which to go on.

Ministers are all too prone to ignore the struggles and worldly problems that afflict their parishioners. Not so John Gare. He could have avoided any mention of the conflict in the valley; but he felt it to be his duty to speak of it. In blunt words he warned them to beware of false prophets. He counselled peace and patience, echoing the very things Montana had advised.

Quantrell had come, bringing his men along. They stood a little apart—a hard-faced crew. Jim felt the big fellow's stare and met his eyes squarely, reading their message of implacable hatred.

If Gare had mentioned Quantrell by name his reference to false prophets could not have been more pointed. The crowd understood him. There was no dissenting murmur. Even the boys who had ridden with Gene gave no sign of disapproval.

"Knowing that I brought the minister from Wild Horse, Quantrell will figure I told him what to say,"

Jim thought. He was little concerned about that. He had sensed a studied coolness on the part of the crowd toward the big fellow. It was almost more than he had dared to hope. He surmised that Quantrell had feared it, otherwise he would hardly have brought his men with him.

The shadows were growing long before the Reverend Gare made his final appeal to them. He quoted from Romans, Chapter 12:

" 'Avenge not yourselves, but rather give place unto wrath: for it is written: Vengeance is mine; I will repay, saith the Lord.

" 'Therefore if thine enemy hunger, feed him; if he thirst, give him drink: for in so doing thou shalt heap coals of fire on his head.' "

In homely words he translated those sentences into a rule of conduct for them.

When he had concluded, the coffin had been placed on the shoulders of Gene's companions and carried to the little dell among the aspens where they stood now. Gare spoke briefly. Catching Dan's eye, he signalled for him to take Mother Crockett back to the house.

The crowd opened up for them to pass. They had almost reached the further edge of it when Mother Crockett saw Quantrell standing before her.

"Come on, Mother," Dan urged softly as he felt her pause. "You'll feel better if you can lie down for a while." Some sixth sense seemed to warn him of what was to occur.

Mother Crockett stopped and levelled her red-rimmed eyes at Quantrell. The crowd held its breath. They saw a harried look flit across his face.

"I'm awful sorry, Mother—" he started to say. Her eyes stopped him.

"Can you give me back my boy?" she demanded stonily. "You took him. But for you he'd be alive this minute."

Dan pleaded with her to continue on to the house.

"You jest got to kinda keep it in, Mother," he said.

Mother Crockett put him off.

"No, Dan'el. I've got sunthin' to say, and there'll never be a better time fer sayin' it." She took in the assembled crowd in a sweeping glance. "You all can lissen to me—you men partic'lar. Most of you are blood kin of mine; so I got a right to speak to you."

There was a tragic deliberation about her that gripped even the children and compelled them to silence.

"We didn't have nuthin' when we come to this valley. By hard work we prospered here. Now we're apt to lose it all; and yet you stand by and let this man turn your heads and our boys' heads with his high and mighty talk about what he's agoin' to do. We knew him when he was freightin' to the Reservation. He had a ranch here then—if you could call it that—but he wa'n't one of us then and he ain't one of us now."

Quantrell couldn't hold his tongue any longer.

"Reckon you're pretty excited, Mother Crockett,"

he exclaimed, trying to hold his voice steady, "but you're heapin' it on a mite strong. The boys shouldn't have done this without me. You know my horse went lame——"

"Too bad he didn't go lame before he fetched you here to-day," Mother Crockett answered stoutly. "I came to Squaw Valley in a covered wagon, with a pot and pan or two, and I'll leave here the same way before I'll see my men folk beholden to you for anythin'. You put one of my boys in his grave, but you're not agoin' to put Brent there. Now you git offen the ranch, and don't ever let me sot eyes on you ag'in!"

John Gare and Montana glanced at each other with peculiar satisfaction. The situation was moving to a climax much sooner than they had supposed possible. Mother Crockett had unwittingly forced a showdown. In a few seconds they would know the true temper of the crowd and exactly where Quantrell stood.

The moment was not without a certain element of danger, although Montana considered it rather remote. He knew there were some among those present who would line up on the big fellow's side. There was evidence that others were through with him. Quantrell's conduct depended on the turn of the balance. If he found the majority against him he would have no alternative but to exit as gracefully as he could. If sentiment favored him, he would remain to make the most of his victory.

It had come so suddenly that it took a moment for

opinions to crystallize. Quantrell essayed a smile of confidence, but his eyes were shifting about uneasily. His men had edged perceptibly nearer him. They were armed—apparently the only ones present who were.

The tension increased as old Lance Morrow stepped forward. In addition to his five sons there were a dozen other Morrows in the valley. As the head of his clan he was a man of importance. Montana considered him the bulwark of Quantrell's strength. If the old man had not openly espoused the big fellow's plans he had, at least, lined up squarely with him on one thing; namely that since this must be a fight to the finish nothing was to be gained by waiting for the other side to bring the fight to them.

Quantrell took confidence. His eyes lost some of their harried look.

"I don't aim to stay where I ain't wanted," he declared with a mirthless grin. "If there's some feeling against me here I reckon I know who I've got to thank. If he can get us quarrellin' among ourselves he'll be doin' just about what he's been plannin' to do all along. Some hard words has been said to me, but I'm big enough to overlook them, though no man likes to feel he's bein' run out. I—I reckon there's no danger of that happenin'——"

To his surprise it failed to win a murmur of approval. Old Lance's eyes had narrowed to slits. Nancy Crockett was his niece and the blood tie outweighed any consideration he might otherwise have shown Quantrell.

"You heard what she said, didn't you, Clay?" he asked, his tone cold and uncompromising. "She asked you to go."

It came as such a complete surprise that Quantrell could not hide his chagrin.

"Hits neither the time ner the place for argufyin'," Lance warned him. "Mebbe you meant well, Clay, but some of us think you went behind our backs in gettin' our boys mixed up in this. We can talk that over later. The thing for you to do now is to go as peaceable as you can."

It was a slap in the face that staggered Quantrell. John Gare had made his way to Montana's side.

"If he blows up there's going to be trouble," he warned Jim. "Be ready for it."

"Don't worry," Jim replied, "Quantrell isn't going to lose his head. He's too cagy for that. A show of temper now and he's in the discard. He'll try to save his face some way. Lance left him a loophole."

The next few seconds saw Jim proved correct. Quantrell strove to dissemble his rage and humiliation. His men didn't know what to make of it.

"Don't worry about me," they heard him say. "I didn't come here to make any trouble. I only wanted to pay my respects to Gene and you, Mother Crockett. I wanted you to know I feel just as bad about this as the rest of you. If I could change places with that boy in his grave yonder I'd do it in a minute. I realize you're all upset now and feel hard toward me; but when you get your second wind and have time to think things over you'll look at it a little different.

"I came into this fight on your side, and I'm goin' through right to the end with you. If ever I can do anythin' to help you, just call on me. Anythin' I got is yours for the askin'."

Mother Crockett, leaning heavily on Dan, waited until Quantrell and his men had started for their horses before she suffered her husband to take her on to the house.

Now that the services were over the crowd made no move to depart. Living apart as they did it was only the burying of a loved one, or perchance a wedding, that permitted them to gather together as they were to-day. The women folk, especially, saw too little of each other. They began to draw apart now, the men moving toward the corral. Knowing that the Reverend Gare would be spending the night with the Crocketts, they looked forward to hearing him speak further. He not only had come a long distance, bringing them the news of Wild Horse and the world beyond, but he had a practical knowledge of husbandry, with all the vexing problems it brought them, even to being able to diagnose the condition of an ailing calf and prescribe the best treatment for tick fever.

Montana had lingered behind, a little bewildered at the turn events had taken. He refused to believe the rebuff Quantrell had just received would deter the big fellow for long.

"But it may trip him at that," he thought, "because it's going to hurry him, whatever his game is. He won't sit around waiting for something to happen."

He was still fifty yards from the house when he saw Quantrell and his men riding toward him, evidently leaving by way of the Skull, although they had ridden in from the north. Jim felt it was a meeting that could accomplish nothing and he chided himself for not having kept out of the man's way. Now that it was unavoidable he met it without fear or favor, continuing on as though Quantrell did not exist.

The big fellow pulled up his horse and threw the animal across Jim's path. There was no need for him to cover up now. His face was livid with rage.

"I can thank you for this," he snarled.

"You can if you care to," Montana answered coolly, "but you may be flattering me."

Quantrell ripped out an oath.

"I'm puttin' it on the fire along with a few other things I got cookin' for you, Montana," he ground out furiously. "I'll be dishin' them out to you one of these days."

"Be careful you don't burn your fingers on 'em," Jim said easily.

He could hear the big fellow cursing as he rode away.

"Got a bad taste in his mouth, all right," Montana

murmured to himself. "You'd have hydrophobia if he bit you tonight."

He found the men grouped about John Gare, listening intently as the minister harangued them. At last the setting sun warned them that they must be getting home. The men began to round up their families. Abel Morrow, one of old Lance's married sons, spoke to Gare.

"Knowin' you was comin'," he said, "we brought the baby over with us. We been aimin' to take him into town to have him christened; but all this trouble comin' up——"

"Why, sure," Gare laughed. "Where is the little slick-ear? I'll put the brand of the Lord on him. You don't want a maverick running around the house."

The mother soon appeared, the women folk trooping after her, and the baby was christened. Immediately afterwards, they began to set out for their homes.

"Fine people, Jim," Gare said as he and Montana sat together on the bench outside the kitchen door. "This country is going to settle up in time and their grandchildren are going to be the ladies and gentlemen of it."

Their conversation drifted to Quantrell.

"You smoked him out," Jim said. "The seed you planted this afternoon bore fruit in a hurry." He was thinking of what Mother Crockett had done.

"Wasn't any more than you've been telling them," Gare insisted.

"They wouldn't take it from me."

"You don't always know what they really think. They respect you, Jim. You've done a lot for them—more than they realize—and you've got small thanks for it. But your day will come. If they win this fight they'll have you to thank."

This was richer praise than Montana felt he deserved. He was saying so when Dan came out to tell them supper was ready.

"I didn't want Mother to speak so sharp to Quantrell," Crockett said to them. "But I've had time to think it over and I'm glad she did. It sorta clears the air."

It was agreed that Brent was to drive Gare back to Wild Horse. Jim took Dan into his confidence regarding his projected trip to the Needles, and in the morning, shortly after Brent and Gare pulled out, he saddled a horse and crossed the Skull. His way lay westward then until he had left even Big Powder Creek far behind. He was climbing steadily.

As usual the high places, with their wide panoramas, fascinated him. He pulled up, and tossing a leg over the horn of his saddle, smoked a contemplative cigarette. What John Gare had said about this country being settled some day came back to him. Sitting there, with a territory almost as large as some of the New England states unrolled before him, he found it hard to believe. And yet, he had seen bench land nesters moving into country back in Idaho that was just as big—plowing the trails under and planting them to wheat.

"Scarcity of water will keep them out of here for a long while," he mused. "A railroad will find it an expensive job throwing a line through these hills. Until that happens this country isn't going to change much."

He had been in sight of the Needles for half an hour, even though they were still eight to ten miles away. He contemplated no difficulty in locating Plenty Eagles and his father. With typical Indian caution, they might have decided that the old cabin was too exposed and not have remained there; but there were only three or four places where they could find water. He was sure to pick up their trail at one of them.

He had just emerged from a patch of scrub cedar and was well across a little mountain meadow, knee-deep in grass, when he jerked his head around and looked back, feeling that he was being watched. He was too far away from the trees to make out anyone lurking there, but well within range of a high-powered rifle. Giving his horse the spurs he soon topped the rise ahead of him. "I'm going to be sure about this," he promised himself. With that in mind he made a circle that would bring him back to the meadow at the point where he had just left it.

It took him a quarter of an hour. He was rewarded by finding the tracks of a shod horse stamped upon those his own pony had made a few minutes past. He slipped out of his saddle and went ahead on foot, his rifle in his hands. He had not gone ten yards before some one hailed him. He raised his eyes to the rocks ahead and saw Plenty Eagles awaiting him.

There was an amused twinkle in the young Indian's eyes. He knew he had surprised Montana.

"Very easy picking you off from up here," he said, his teeth gleaming whitely as he grinned.

"I knew I wasn't alone," Jim smiled. "But why are you trailing me?"

"Not knowing it is you until you cross the meadow. My pony stumble in the brush." He permitted himself a chuckle. "You hearing him all right," he declared. "You move fast; pretty soon you hard to find."

"I just lit out on a little circle to find out what was what," Jim acknowledged.

"Not good for circle down-hill," said Plenty Eagles. "Me, if I was Quantrell, be just too bad for you. Thinking you more careful."

"I guess it was a tenderfoot trick," Jim was compelled to admit. "What's this about Quantrell? Has he been up here?"

Plenty Eagles shook his head. He had been down below repeatedly, watching Quantrell, but he had no intention of admitting it.

"Just thinking you better be watching out for him," he said. "Not seeing any one up here except a Bar S man and a girl."

It startled Montana, but as he stared at the young Indian understanding dawned in his eyes.

"A girl?" he queried. "You mean Letty Stall?"

"Same one who was in Wild Horse with the old man," Plenty Eagles explained.

"Rode in from Willow Vista," Jim thought, his mouth unusually grave as he considered the dangers to which she was now exposed. It passed belief that Mr. Stall had given permission for her to come. She had made this decision herself.

He told himself she was being foolhardy; and yet, it was no more than he could have expected. He could surmise the reasons that had prompted her to come— and it did not occur to him that he figured in them at all.

"When did you see her?" he asked.

"Day before yesterday. I follow them for long time. Know you not wanting anything happen to her."

Montana was not prepared for such shrewd obser- vation. He could feel his ears burning. Gratitude tem- pered his annoyance; the boy had done him a service.

"You did well, *Cola*," he said and then turned the conversation abruptly by asking about the boy's father.

"Oh, he liking this place," said Plenty Eagles. "Not staying on cabin. Make wickiup by Antelope Springs —you know that place, eh?"

Jim said that he did.

"All the time when my father young man coming

there for hunt," the boy went on. "Still some meat up here."

"I've got some grub for you," Montana informed him. "I was over in Wild Horse a day ago. Rand and I got a bagful of things together for you."

Long experience with Indians had taught him that gratitude usually rendered them inarticulate. Months later, when he had quite forgotten some trifling favor, he had often been reminded that they had not forgotten.

It was so now. The young Piute just grinned, and obviously embarrassed, turned to find his pony.

"I want to make talk with your father," Montana told him. His blood was flowing faster. He found a new tang in the air. It was strange that the mere presence of Letty Stall in Squaw Valley could so affect one who believed himself so far removed from her thoughts.

With Plenty Eagles leading the way they rode on. Jim was satisfied to trail along with his thoughts for company. When they reached the old cabin below the Needles, he saw the Piute draw up and wait for him.

"You still thinking my father know somethings about who killed your friend, eh?" he asked without preamble of any sort. Montana purposely withheld his answer for a moment.

"I think he does," he said finally. "From his perch up there at the mine he could see what went on below him. Being afraid that Quantrell or his men might find his hide-out, he'd have been watching them particularly. . . . Have you been talking to him?"

"Yeh, but so old man hard to make him understand." Plenty Eagles pressed his knees into his horse and went on. It put such an abrupt end to their conversation that Montana wondered about it.

"Doesn't look as though he was going to help me very much," he thought, giving the boy a shrewd glance. "Something worrying him. He wants to talk, but he's afraid."

They found old Thunder Bird basking in the sun. Jim raised his hand to sign to him that he came as a friend. The old brave's wrinkled face remained an inscrutable mask.

Plenty Eagles spoke to his father in Piute.

"*Ai*—" the old man grunted.

"Telling him you came to have big talk with him," the boy explained to Montana.

"No hurry about that," said Jim. To prove it he told Plenty Eagles to take the bag he had brought and then proceeded to yank the saddle from his pony. When he had spread a blanket he began to draw forth from the bag the treasures he had brought. Old Thunder Bird's face lighted up when Montana placed before him a pound of tobacco.

"Tobacco . . . good!" he grinned.

"And here's a new pipe to go with it," Jim went on, as pleased as the old man. He had brought sugar, coffee, flour and a side of bacon, but it was the sight of a can of syrup that completely broke down Thunder Bird's reserve. He picked up the little cabin-shaped can and fondled it as a child does a toy.

"Never paying you for all this," Plenty Eagles declared solemnly.

"*Cola*, my heart is full for you and your father; so is Rand's, yet you talk of paying us. I come to your wickiup to spread the robe and smoke the pipe, and we are one."

He found the old man more pliable than he was the day he had taken him from the mine. It was not always possible for him to understand whether Thunder Bird understood him, even though he regarded him intently, trying to read the little fleeting glimpses of emotion that flitted across his weather-beaten face.

He talked at length, moving to his point by indirection. After he had told them about Gene Crockett's death, he touched the subject that had brought him there. Immediately Plenty Eagles addressed his father. Jim would put a question and the boy would talk to Thunder Bird. If the old man answered at all it was to his son.

Montana understood a few Piute expressions but he could not follow them. He felt he was not getting anywhere. Half an hour passed without producing the slightest information.

"Too old," the boy shrugged. "Not remember so much."

Jim hid his sense of failure. The thought had grown

on him that Plenty Eagles was really keeping the old man from telling what he knew. When he had spoken to Thunder Bird before the old man had been able to make himself understood without his son's help.

He said nothing at the time but ate a bite with them and after smoking a cigarette or two prepared to leave. He said farewell to the old man, and, accompanied by Plenty Eagles, started for the valley. When they reached the cabin, the boy pulled up. He was turning back there. Montana had waited for this moment.

"Plenty Eagles—why are you afraid to let your father talk to me?"

"Not afraid," he said.

"*Cola,* your tongue is not straight now," Jim chided him. "I can read your eyes, and I know what I say is true. You have talked to your father and he has told you what I want to know." Montana was only voicing a surmise. The effect it produced in the boy prompted him to continue. "My heart bleeds for your father. I will not see him go hungry. When the winter comes he will be warm. Nothing he could tell me would bring trouble to him."

It moved the boy.

"It is true," Plenty Eagles murmured. "He has spoken. If I am afraid it is for him."

"I promise you no trouble will come to him," Jim repeated. " . . . Was it Quantrell?"

"Not knowing that. It was so: My father is hiding

in the mine. Quantrell and some of his men are there; building the gate. A man comes and tells them there is Bar S men in the cañon. Quantrell he say, 'This what we been wait for. We start ball rolling now.' "

"Yes—" Jim prompted. "What did they do?"

"They riding away together. My father is watch. He see them come out on the rimrocks. In few minutes he hear a rifle. They come back, then; but Quantrell is not with them."

"No, he went on to the meeting at the Box C," Montana muttered. If he had needed proof to convince him that what Rand and Gare and he had been thinking was true he had it now.

"The chance they had been waiting for," he mused bitterly. "A chance to start the ball rolling—to make the fight a certainty by killing Billy!"

He realized that he would likely never know who actually shot the boy. But here, as in the case with Gene, the crime could be placed at Quantrell's door.

"I'll never forget this, Plenty Eagles," he said. "You are my brother."

"Quantrell no good," the young Indian murmured thoughtfully. "Better you let me kill him before he make more trouble. . . . I have plenty chance."

Montana knew the depth of the feeling that had prompted the boy to speak. He put his hand on Plenty Eagles' shoulder.

"You get that idea out of your mind, *Cola*," he said. "This is sorta up to me."

"I be watching him just the same."

"I don't object to that. If you run into something that looks queer, you get word to me. He's angling for something, and he can't get it without showing his hand."

CHAPTER XV

LONG RIDERS

WHEN Brent Crockett returned from Wild Horse he brought a letter from Graham Rand. Rand wrote he had talked to Vickers, the new agent, and had not got anything further out of him. The man had left for Vale. But he was often up there, and Graham did not consider it had anything to do with the Squaw Valley sale. He concluded in characteristic fashion:

"Undoubtedly I've been worrying you about nothing at all. So forget it. If I keep on this way I'll soon be taking in knitting. I'll manage to keep you posted— about Vickers and not the knitting."

There was an apparent contradiction there that struck Montana at once. He could smile over Graham's letter, but his fears were not allayed. The days that immediately followed brought no new threat from above the North Fork, and a dozen times Jim wondered if their inactivity had any connection with news from Washington.

Quantrell did not come to the Box C again. One

evening Brent rode over to Lance Morrow's place. He came back with word that Quantrell had been there, talking to the old man. He claimed to have had an offer from Stall and Matlack for his property.

"He told Lance that he'd turned it down," Brent informed them. "Claims he'll never sell out to the Bar S."

"Don't you believe it!" Montana scoffed! "He'd sell out in a hurry if he got an offer—and the price was attractive. I'd have to see the offer in writing before I'd admit he had one."

Crockett disagreed with him.

"That's goin' pritty far, Jim," he argued. "I ain't got no love for Quantrell, but I'm not goin' to let that run away with my judgment. If they could grab Quantrell's place it would be just puttin' on the vise a little tighter. I've never said nothin' but I've wondered once or twice if somethin' like that wouldn't happen. I don't see why you figure they wouldn't make him an offer. What's your argument?"

"Dollars and cents! I never knew Henry Stall to give a man a profit when he had the whiphand. Quantrell's got some water, but it's hard to get at. He's been frozen out of the Big Powder. It just don't make sense to me, Dan."

"Just the same it would be a blow to us if Quantrell sold out," Crockett murmured glumly. "It would be pritty discouragin'. First thing you know someone else would be takin' the bait. You got to give the devil his due, Jim. Think what you will about the man, but if he sticks with us we got to be big enough to appreciate it."

Jim let it go at that. Despite all that had happened he could see that Dan still had some faith in Quantrell. Undoubtedly the others had, too.

"If you talk loud enough and long enough you certainly can fool a lot of people," he summed up to himself.

With Gene gone there was more work for all hands. A brief hour of relaxation after supper and they were ready for bed.

One evening late in the week Jubal Stark rode in. There was an air of being the carrier of important news about him.

"Well, I guess they're at it ag'in," he declared. "They're runnin' off our stock now."

Crockett put down his Bible.

"You mean that, Jubal?"

"Course I mean it!" his visitor exclaimed with asperity. "They cut out ten or twelve head of Quantrell's yearlin's yesterday. To-day they were in my stuff. I jest thought I'd warn you as I have the others."

Mother Crockett came into the kitchen. Jubal was her cousin. His news had to be repeated to her.

"What you said the other day about leavin' here in a covered wagon, Nancy, is jest what we'll be doin', I reckin," Jubal declared. "They burned down my house and now they're runnin' off my stock. I tell you things is gittin' desperrit. Hits all right to talk about the Lord havin' his vengeance, but I don't figger we're supposed to let another outfit rob us blind."

"But what makes you so certain the Bar S got your yearlings?" Jim asked. He knew he was venturing on dangerous ground in putting the question to a man as bitter and excited as Jubal Stark. He saw him bristle with indignation.

"Don't you come any of that on me, Jim!" he exclaimed angrily. "I wouldn't put anythin' past that bunch! Old man Stall is out to break us, and he don't care how he does hit!"

"He'll run you out if he can, but he won't steal your cattle."

Crockett shook his head hopelessly.

"I don't know, Jim," he said. "It's hard to believe, but who else could be doin' it?"

"It's up to us to find out. Give a rustler a little rope and he'll trip himself every time."

He felt nothing was to be gained by voicing the suspicion that was surging through his mind. He had been waiting for Quantrell to show his hand. Here was his play. As Montana put together the pieces of the puzzle that had been intriguing him for days he knew there could be little doubt of it.

"They'd likely run me out of the valley if I said what I'm thinking," he admitted to himself. "It's a case of catching Quantrell with the goods now."

The following day Joe Gault reported that the

rustlers had taken toll from him. It happened repeatedly. The men met one afternoon at Lance Morrow's ranch. Montana went with Dan. He was not surprised to find Quantrell there, talking as loud as ever.

A dozen men spoke. Every one accused the Bar S. They were in no mood to listen to anything to the contrary.

"You were told to wait until they brought the fight to you," Quantrell declared, his eyes seeking Jim. "Well, it's here now, ain't it? You got what you were waitin' for. "What are you goin' to do about it?"

"There's only one thing to do," Joe Gault called out. "We got to hit back. Cattle can be raided north of the Fork just as easy as below."

"That's plain talk," Jubal Stark said. "It's what we should do. Them that thinks so step this way!"

Some hesitated, but it was only for a moment or two, until Dan and Montana stood alone.

"If you feel they're right—that it's the thing to do —you join 'em, Dan," Jim advised. "I don't want you to hold back on my account."

The others were listening.

"No," Dan said thoughtfully, "I'm not ready for that yet. I never rustled another man's stuff, and I ain't agoin' to begin now. I've fought cattle thieves before and wiped 'em out without turnin' rustler myself. You know where the law is in this country; it ain't on our side. If I catch a man with one of my steers in his possession I'll know what to do; so will you. We got to sleep on our rifles and ride these rustlers down. We can do it if we pull together. Until we've tried it and failed we shouldn't be thinkin' of turnin' thief."

They were the sanest words that had been uttered there, and although Quantrell decried them and Jubal Stark insisted on fighting fire with fire, the meeting broke up with the understanding that, for the present, as many as could would meet every evening at Jubal's ranch and ride until dawn.

It was a victory for Crockett, but Jim felt they were wasting their time. Quantrell was a party to their deliberations and could easily avoid them.

True to what Jim had predicted to himself, they rode for three nights without encountering anyone. Quantrell and some of his men rode with them. It seemed to have the desired effect; no more stock was run off.

Dan was about to congratulate himself on their success when the rustlers moved across the Reservation. The blow fell heaviest on the Box C.

"They must have got fifty head of my best yearlin's," he computed after a careful checking. He returned to the house and refused to speak to anyone. By supper time he had himself in hand.

"I reckon I was wrong, Jim," he said. We've got to give them the same medicine they're givin' us. You can't say I haven't been patient. I wanted to be fair, but I'm at the end of my rope."

"A rope is what we ought to have around their necks," said Brent.

"I know how you feel," Jim declared. "You're fighting the Bar S so it's only natural for you to lay your troubles to them; but I'm no more ready to believe right now that Henry Stall would run an iron on another man's stuff than I was a week ago. He might cheat you legally, but this is just a cut beneath him. I'm not going to say anything more. You do as you think best, Dan, and I'll string along with you."

They were out day and night now, working in shifts. It was no easy task for two or three men to ride herd in an unfenced country like that and see everything.

In the early afternoon, after they had been in to water, the cattle would move back into the hills. You couldn't keep them in sight always.

Early the following week, Montana was on the day shift with old Ben. Taking it for granted that the cattle were safe enough out in the open, he had left Ben on the Skull and climbed the rocky saddle that fell away to the Big Powder on the west and the Skull to the east. Stretched out in the mahogany brush, he had an unobstructed view of the country east and west. Below him was a steep cutbank.

A faint breeze rustled the sage. The blue sky was cloudless. His horse grazed a short way off.

It was a day for dreaming. He was not roused out of his lethargy until he caught a brief glimpse of four horsemen to the north. They were on the same ridge with him and moving his way.

It was enough to make him sit up alertly. They were too far away to make recognition possible.

"This may be interesting," he mused. "If they aren't trying to hide out they'll get off the ridge before they get down this far."

Although he continued to scrutinize the hills and the draws, he failed to get another glance at them. Twenty minutes passed, time enough for them to have hove into view.

"They must be down below," he thought. He crawled up to the edge of the cutbank and scanned the country beneath him. He quickly located the four men. They were following an old cow trail through the high sage. In a few moments he recognized Quantrell, Shorty and two others who had been among the bunch at the mine that day. The trail they were following would bring them directly beneath him in ten to fifteen minutes.

Montana could not repress a grunt of satisfaction. His suspicions were rapidly crystallizing into fact. Four men, off their own range, skulking through the brush was almost circumstantial evidence enough to convict, with things as they stood.

Their manner was tense and furtive. They were almost below Montana when Quantrell raised his hand and called a halt.

"We'll hole up here for an hour," he said. "After we hobble the horses, we'll climb this bank and lay out."

With the odds four to one against him, Jim knew he had to make his presence known while the advantage of his position was still in his favor.

"Come on, sit steady!" he called out. "And mighty careful with the hands!"

The gleaming of his rifle barrel told them where to find him. Quantrell's mouth fell open in dismay for a moment.

"You're taking a mighty big chance, aren't you?" Jim drawled chillingly. "You're a long ways from your own range. Can't be looking for strays to-day."

Quantrell found his tongue. "Don't give me any of your lip!" he bellowed. "We got tipped off that we might find a couple of Bar S hands down this way. Reckon we almost found one."

It won a mocking laugh from Montana.

"The next time you get tipped off to anything you want to have witnesses," he said. "Now you turn your horses toward the Powder and get across. If you don't move fast enough to suit me, I'll find a way to hurry you up a little. *Vamos, señors!*"

They went. Three hundred yards away, Quantrell glanced back. "I'd like to pick him off up there!" he growled. "I wonder how much he heard?"

"Enough," Shorty muttered viciously. "We sure stubbed our toe that time. The quicker we git him the better off we'll be."

"You said it!" Quantrell agreed. "The best thing we can do is to start talkin' about it before he gets the chance. We can circle back east of the creek below Stark's place. We'll stop there and chin a little. Montana can't prove anythin'."

Jim watched them until they were across the Big Powder.

"There goes your rustlers," he muttered. "If they'd only gone on a quarter of a mile instead of pulling up right here, I'd have caught them red-handed. . . . I wonder what Dan's going to say about this."

Crockett was too surprised to have anything to say for a few moments.

They talked for an hour.

"It gets to this," Jim concluded. "Quantrell has set us at each other's throats. I happen to know that his outfit got Billy Sauls. I didn't say anything at the time, but the day after Jubal Stark's house burned, I trailed a rider almost to Quantrell's range before I lost the tracks. Every move he's made has looked queer to me. Look at his outfit. How can he afford to hire seven or eight men?"

"It don't look right," Dan admitted.

"I'll say it don't. If I could have got off that bank this afternoon without giving myself away I would have had proof enough for you. I tell you, Dan, you don't know for a fact that Bar S has ever had a man south of the North Fork. Quantrell has always been rushing you into trouble. While you were fighting each other he was going to run off with the cream. He's been doing just that. The nights he rode with you no stock was run off. When he had you scouring the country south of the Fork he slipped down into the Reservation and did his stuff. It was a pretty safe game."

"Well, I don't know what to think," Dan declared. "I want to be right this time. You said something about knowing that his bunch got Billy Sauls. You mind sayin' how you know?"

"It's breaking a confidence to tell you, but I know it's safe enough with you. I told you why I went to the Needles. Well, I got the information I was after. Old Thunder Bird's story would convict them in any court."

Montana's patience was wearing thin. He crushed his cigarette between his fingers and tossed it away.

"You say you don't know what to think, Dan," he went on. "Well, I'm asking you—do you believe Quantrell was way down in the Reservation, on your range, looking for a Bar S man in the middle of the afternoon? Hobbling their horses and laying out! Laying out for what? Why did they want to hole up right there? You know why! Your steers were just below the saddle!"

Dan communed with himself for a moment.

"There ain't nothin' else to think," he said gravely. "He's guilty as hell!"

"You bet he is! There's only one thing more I want to know."

"What's that?"

"If the Bar S hasn't been losing stuff, too. If they have, the case against Quantrell is complete. I aim to find out, Dan. I'm going up there in the morning and see the old man himself."

"Lord sakes, Jim, don't be a fool!" Crockett exclaimed. "Why, if you're caught comin' or goin' you'll have some explainin' to do! It would look like you *were* double-crossin' us, jest as Quantrell has been sayin'. You'd be lucky if you didn't find a rope around your neck!"

"It's a chance, but I'm going to take it. It will mean a lot to you and I reckon it will mean even more to me."

Chapter XVI

DANGEROUS GROUND

DAN CROCKETT tried to dissuade Montana from trying to see old Slick-ear.

"Somethin's sure to happen to you, and I don't want to feel responsible, Jim," he pleaded. "Suppose we say nothin' fer a day or so about your having seen Quantrell. He may come again."

"You don't savvy him at all, Dan, if you think that," Montana disagreed. "I'm on my own in going up the Big Powder. I could have killed Quantrell yesterday and have gone free for it. But that wouldn't satisfy me. I'm going to tumble him into the dust before I step on him. If I can talk to Mr. Stall I can hurry that day along."

He went back to the Reservation to relieve old Ben for a few hours. Later, without any sleep, he set out for the north. By daylight he was at the forks. He tarried awhile. Nothing had changed since he had last been there. Half an hour later he continued up the Big Powder.

Once well across the Bar S line, he climbed out of the creek bottom and took up a point of vantage where he could command a view of the creek. Cattle were moving in to water. He knew someone would be along shortly. It was safer to wait and hail a man than to walk into trouble. It was his intention to ask for safe conduct to the house.

The morning wore on, however, without bringing anyone. He had been waiting over three hours when he caught the sound of a shod hoof below. The rider crossed a break in the willows. He saw then that it was Letty Stall.

Even though he knew she was in Squaw Valley, meeting her so unexpectedly shook him out of his habitual calm. Unconsciously a sigh escaped him. He had told himself countless times that she was as far removed from him as the stars and quite as unattainable. And yet, mere sight of her was enough to unnerve him.

He hardly supposed her to be alone, two or three miles from the house. He waited, expecting to see a Bar S man ride into the open; but Letty had crossed the break and no one rode after her. It was only a minute before he saw her again.

"Wouldn't think Reb would let her come down this far alone," he thought. "She still rides well." Inevitably, memory of their long rides together at Willow Vista came back to him.

Undoubtedly, she would resent his intrusion, but he felt there was too much at stake to hang back. With his heart beating rapidly, he retraced his way to the creek bottom and walked his horse out into the open.

Letty saw him presently. The color left her cheeks as she recognized him. Jim reined in beside her and swept off his hat.

"Ma'am, you shouldn't come down so far. It isn't safe."

Letty found him thinner than usual, but self-conscious as always in her presence. It pleased her to pretend an aloofness she was far from feeling.

"You are trespassing, not I," she said, her blue eyes inscrutable. "I didn't know you were making war on women. I thought you were confining yourself to men and cattle and destroying other people's range."

"I reckon you've got a pretty hard opinion of me," he murmured unhappily. "Folks don't always see things alike. What I've done I did because I thought it was right. There's been killing and destroying of property on both sides. It hasn't been any of my doing. I know what you folks up here think of me. It isn't so much different down below. I seem to be taking it on two sides."

"That's the usual fate of martyrs, isn't it?" she queried. "I suppose you realize you might have some trouble explaining your presence here if Reb or the men found you. They have orders to shoot first and inquire afterwards. Something has to be done to stop this rustling."

She saw him stiffen at the word.

"That's why I am here," he declared frankly. "I wanted to find out if you were losing stock, too. This fight can be stopped. I've got to see your father, ma'am. If he'll talk to me, something may come of it."

His sincerity touched her. In the face of all that had happened, she still believed in him, despite her father's enmity.

"He'll not be pleased to see you," she told him. "He holds you responsible for all his difficulties here in Squaw Valley."

Montana did not surmise how staunchly she had defended him against her father's attacks, or to what lengths she had gone to remain in the valley.

"I suppose he thinks we are rustling his cattle."

"Naturally——"

"And down below they think he's getting our stuff. Can't you see how absurd it is? I've got to talk to him, ma'am!"

"He's at the house," she said. "I can't promise you much, but if you'll tighten my mare's cinch I'll take you to him."

Jim slipped out of his saddle and helped her down. She felt his hand tremble on her arm. For a moment their eyes met. A sigh escaped her. It would only have taken a word for them to have reached an understanding. But Jim looked away to hide his embarrassment.

"Like old times, isn't it?" she murmured hurriedly. "But then, I don't suppose you ever think of them."

"I do, ma'am," he said awkwardly. If she only knew how often he thought of them!

"Letty is my name," she murmured, her eyes glowing with mischief. "You used to call me Letty—when we were alone."

Jim gave the cinch a savage tug. He was suffering exquisite torture. Letty suspected it and was happy. A hundred little things told her he loved her and was too shy to say it.

"It's—dangerous down here," he said. "You don't often ride so far alone, do you?"

"Hardly," Letty smiled, thinking of the subterfuges she had to use to get out of sight of the house. "Father says I shouldn't be here at all."

"That's one thing we can agree on," Jim murmured.

"Oh—you're not glad to see me then?"

"I—I'm awfully happy to see you, Letty. It's just that I don't want you to get into trouble. . . . I knew you were here."

Letty's eyes sobered as a thought disturbed her.

"Then you've been up before——"

"No. Someone saw you when you came in—beyond the Needles. This is only the second time I've set foot on Bar S range. The other time I—had a few words with Reb."

"I know about that," Letty murmured softly. "I love the way you belittle it. I thought it was very brave of you to come over and get that boy, knowing you were apt to be killed."

"Someone had to come. . . . I don't suppose it set very well with your father."

Letty laughed lightly.

"You know him too well to make that question necessary," she said.

"I guess that's so," Jim answered moodily. "Everything I do seems calculated to make hard feelings between us. After Wild Horse and the trouble here I wasn't any too sure you'd speak to me. I figure a man has to play the game as he sees it. Sometimes I wonder if I did the right thing by getting into this fight. Then again, when I see what losing it is going to mean to them, I'm glad I did."

"I'm afraid they are going to lose," Letty mused aloud. "Father seems so cocksure lately."

"He'll find them hard to whip."

"That's the pity of it, isn't it, Jim?" Her eyes were wistful. "I know the mother of that boy will never forgive us. They must hate us. . . . But there was Billy——"

"They had nothing to do with that, Letty. Billy was murdered. . . . I'll be settling that before long."

"You know who did it?"

"I know, all right. That's just another reason why I want to see your father. I can set him right about several things."

Letty was suddenly silent. Jim was conscious of it.

"Maybe you'd like to be going," he said. "I'll help you up."

She shook her head.

"Jim—I don't want you to get in trouble over Billy.

It would be so easy for something to happen. . . . I couldn't stand that——"

A pleasant feeling of confusion stole through Montana. He could feel the pulse in his throat throbbing violently.

"Reckon nothing's going to happen," he was finally able to say. "When the showdown comes you couldn't expect me to walk away from it. I'm sorry I mentioned it; but I'm pretty full of this thing." In an effort to turn the conversation into pleasanter channels he asked about Willow Vista.

"Hasn't changed a bit since you left," she murmured absent-mindedly. She knew his code; its glorious courage and the quixotic, even absurd, inhibitions it placed on him. Undoubtedly he had said he would avenge Billy. Having said it he would go through with it, regardless of danger, believing his self-respect depended on keeping his word. Nothing she could say would dissuade him.

"You still ride that big *savenna* I broke for you?" he asked.

"I've got him down in California now. I call him Mesquite."

"He should have developed into quite a horse."

"He has. We're great pals. In the winter, when I know I'll not be coming back to the desert for months, I get all choked up with loneliness. I tell Mesquite all about it. He seems to understand. Guess he gets lonesome for the high places, too, sometimes. You never get away from this country, so you don't know how homesick the smell of sage-brush can make you. Mr. Tracey shipped me a box full last fall. You should have seen Mesquite's ears stand up when he got a whiff of it."

Jim decided the conversation had not taken a more pleasant course. The thought of Letty Stall, down in California, surrounded by the luxury her father provided, among cultured men, so unlike himself, made her seem even more remote.

He helped her into her saddle and fell in beside her, stealing sly little glances at her mobile lips and softly curving throat. It was like old times, siding her over the hills. It almost made him forget the serious mission that brought him there.

From across the creek, two men watched them until they passed out of sight. They had been watching Montana for half an hour. The little red-haired one glared at the big man at his side.

"Why'd you knock my gun down, Clay?" he demanded angrily. "I could 'a' picked him off easy!"

"This'll be better, Shorty," Quantrell replied, venomously. "I said he was a Bar S man—and this proves it! Stuck on that girl, sure as Fate! You saw him moonin' over her, didn't yuh? I call this good!" A puzzled look settled on the big fellow's face. "You know I was only talkin' when I claimed he was still workin' for old man Stall; but I'm damned now if I don't believe I hit the nail on the head! That girl of his was in Wild Horse, and now she shows up in the valley, where a women shouldn't be. What do you make of it if it isn't a case of her father knowin' Montana's soft for her and havin' her on hand to play him for a sucker?"

"Sounds like sense to me," Shorty agreed.

"It sure is a break for us. We'll go back to about a mile this side of the Forks. You can go up to the house and get the boys. I'll round up Joe Gault and half a dozen others and meet you there on the creek. I want 'em to get an eye-full of this bird on his way down. The way they're feelin' now they'll jerk the air out of that meddlin' fool and we'll be through with him."

This was cunning that Shorty could appreciate.

"We don't want to lose any time," Quantrell reminded him. "Can't tell how long he'll be up there."

When he and Shorty parted he climbed out of the creek bottom and took to the hills. He failed to find Gault at home, but Joe's wife told him he was over at Jubal Stark's ranch. Cursing the delay, Quantrell rode away at a punishing pace. When he reached his destination he was rewarded by finding several others present—Dave Morrow, young Lance and Jubal's brother-in-law, Galen Stroud.

The situation was one made to order for Quantrell. His news came as a bombshell.

"The two-faced skunk!" Jubal bellowed. "I'm fer stringin' him up! All his soft talk about waitin'! You can see what he's after now, can't you? Wanted us to sit still and do nuthin' till they'd plucked us clean!"

All were bitter and expressed themselves accordingly.

"I'm for makin' an example of him," Gault said. "He's made a fool out of me, for I always had confidence in him; I thought he was right. It's easy to see he's been takin' us over from the start. We better get our horses and ride."

When they reached the point on the Big Powder where Quantrell and Shorty had parted they found him and the rest of the big fellow's outfit already on hand. Shorty said Montana had not come down the creek.

"We're here in time then," Quantrell muttered. Back at Stark's place he had let the others do the talking. He was taking the lead now. "We don't know which side of the creek he'll take," he told them. "Me and the boys will lay out on the other side; you can stay here. He'll be right on us before he smells trouble. Better tie the horses to be sure they won't be moving about to tip him off."

"Just remember that we want to take him alive," Stark called out as Quantrell and his men started across the creek. "We ain't agoin' to end this with enythin' as easy on him as a bullet."

"You said somethin'!" Quantrell rasped. "We got a few things to choke down his throat first."

The spot he had chosen for the ambush suited their purpose ideally. The willows grew dense there. When they had crawled into them and concealed themselves there was no sign to say that danger lurked there.

But they were totally unaware of a pair of piercing black eyes watching them from the top of the bank just as intently as they were watching the creek bottom for sight of Montana. It was Plenty Eagles. Quantrell had made few moves in the last few days that the young Indian had not observed. He could not voice his gratitude to Jim, but he was proving it in more tangible ways.

When he finally slipped away, he moved noiselessly. No eye was turned in his direction. After he had put a screen of trees between him and the waiting men, he came back to the creek bottom and headed for the north.

"Not letting Montana walk into that trap," he muttered fiercely. "He make big mistake not letting me kill Quantrell."

CHAPTER XVII

SPEAKING OF MISTAKES

MR. STALL had said nothing to Letty concerning the reason for his mysterious journey to Vale with MacMasters. He had returned breathing confidence regarding the outcome of the struggle in which he was engaged.

Reb had met him with the news that parties unknown were rustling their cattle. It was rubbing him on a sore spot.

"It's squarely up to you to spot it," old Slick-ear had raged. "You ought to know where to look for them."

"I'm only askin' permission to shoot first and ask questions later," Reb had answered.

"On our range, yes! That's first principles in this business! Have you seen any one?"

"Last night—but they got away. . . . I'm not under-estimatin' Jim Montana now. He's pretty smart."

The shot told. Mr. Stall chewed his mustache.

"You may have to look further than Montana, Mr. Russell."

"Mebbe he isn't leadin' 'em," Reb hedged, "But he's

standin' for it; he's still down there. It gets to the same thing with me."

Despite renewed vigilance on his part the rustling had continued. Mr. Stall stormed to no avail. In his mind he charged up every lost steer against the day when the Squaw Valley men should be forced to their knees.

Although he never admitted it, he was secretly happy to have Letty near him. Her "sprained" ankle had improved slowly and before she had fully recovered he had ceased thinking about sending her away.

Weeks had passed since he had visited his Nevada ranches. Business in California called to him. Only by mail could he keep in touch with his far-flung empire. He would write for half a day at a time, putting out of his mind all thought of the Squaw Valley strife and giving orders and advice to his foremen, with an eye for detail that was uncanny.

He was at it today, dispatching a long letter to the foreman of his Humboldt ranch, east of Winnemucca.

"I am in receipt of your report for last month. In general it is satisfactory. I note what you say about the men. Tom Kelsey has been working for me a long time, but if he insists on going into Golconda and getting drunk, you should dismiss him. It has a bad effect on the rest of the men, and you can't get work out of him if he's been drunk the night before.

I notice in your accounts the amount of meat

you have been using. It is altogether too much. I want the men to have enough; but you have a good garden on the river. The men will work better for having more vegetables and less meat.

Of course it is disappointing to learn that Mrs. Kirk did not come up to your expectations as a cook. I have found that when you have to hire a man and his wife to get a cook you are usually borrowing trouble. Either the man will not do the chores or work with a will at anything, or his wife will turn out to be a very third-rate woman in the kitchen. I advise you to hire a Chinaman. They are clean and waste very little.

I had been waiting to visit the ranch to tell you about the stove in the dining-room. The legs are wobbly, and if some one bumps against the stove accidentally it will surely upset. I want you to have that looked after while the stove is not in use. A fire would be very expensive.

In regard to the cellar. The dobe was crumbling badly last year. It would be a waste of money to repair it. You will find it more economical to build a new one. You could place it next to the blacksmith shop.

I cannot say when I will be down. I note that Mr. Taylor would like to contract for some of our pasture this fall. With the water situation what it is, I am against that. We will need all our pasture, and there is no profit in letting it out and having to repair the fences and possibly pump water for him."

A broken window, a leaking head-gate in an irrigation ditch—nothing was too small to escape his attention. Perhaps it would not have been unusual for a man to give such attention to details on one ranch, but he was doing it for a score of ranches spread over four states.

When thus engaged he was so absorbed with his train of thought that he permitted no interruption except on the most urgent matters. Even Letty, for all her bossing of him, respected his wish in this matter.

He had seen her ride away that morning. But she had been doing it for some days now and always returning within an hour or so, and it gave him no cause for concern this time. Several hours had passed as he sat at his desk, but he wrote on unmindful of her protracted absence.

If he had stepped to the door he could have caught a glimpse of her, riding in from the south with Montana beside her.

Blissfully unaware of the fact that they had been spied on, Jim and Letty had followed the Big Powder north. It gave Montana a thrill to see the old Bar S on a steer's hide. It was like coming home, in a way.

Reb had too many men riding the range for Jim and Letty to proceed very far before encountering them. They had not covered more than a mile before Johnny Lefleur cut across their trail. Seeing Jim there was startling enough to leave Johnny speechless.

Letty called out a greeting to him, but Montana maintained a tight-lipped silence. He knew he was *persona non grata* with all Bar S men. He did not propose to give Johnny a chance to humble him.

They rode on. Letty had lost her smile. For a few minutes she had been day-dreaming, but the work-a-day world with its problems and strife had caught up with her.

They met other men who turned away without a word, contempt for Montana in their eyes.

"Don't let it worry you, ma'am," Jim told her. "I had to expect that or worse."

They had just reached the ranch yard when a horseman rode toward them. It was Reb. After his first start of surprise, a sneer curled his lips and he turned away without a word. Montana pretended not to notice.

"I'll hardly be seeing you before you leave," Letty told him. "I want you to know this, Jim. If there's ever anything I can do to help—I will! You'll find Father in the front room."

She was gone then, without another word.

Old Slick-ear was seated at a table, his pen still travelling swiftly over the paper as he dashed off another of his endless letters. Jim stood there for half a minute before the old man looked up. The change that swept over Mr. Stall's plump face was startling. With a snort of rage he pushed his chair back.

"What you doing here?" he demanded.

"I came to see you, Mr. Stall."

"Well, you're seeing me! How did you get here?"

Jim hesitated. "Miss Letty brought me——"

"That girl!" The old man's face was purple. He slammed his pen down on the table violently. It splattered ink across his letter.

Montana explained how he had met Letty and begged her to bring him to the house.

"Well, you're here now, and you can turn around and get out! If you think you can come here as an envoy from that cattle-stealing pack you've been running with, you're mistaken!"

"But we're losing stuff, too, Mr. Stall—perhaps more than you—and you're not taking it!"

"Hunh?" Suspicion and baffled rage battled for supremacy in that hoarse cry.

"And we are not rustling your stuff!" Jim drove on. "I'll prove that to you if you'll listen. Don't get the idea I'm here asking for quarter, or speaking for anyone but myself. This fight can go on, but while we're battling over the bone, a third party is running off with it!"

It was unexpected enough to take some of the bluster out of the old man. Keen judge of men that he was, he knew Montana was not given to over-statement. He stared at him fiercely but he could not beat down his eyes.

"What do you mean by that?" he demanded, and he could not have clipped the words off shorter with a knife.

"I mean that Billy Sauls wasn't killed in any range

feud. He was murdered in the hope that it would stampede Reb into something just as desperate. For the same reason, houses and hay were burned—and the work charged to you."

Old Slick-ear bit at his mustache for a moment and then did a typical about-face.

"Sit down," he said, his tone almost mild.

"No, I'll get this off my chest standing up. I'm too full of it to sit down. I should have tumbled to the game long before I left Wild Horse. I *was* suspicious, but I never got it right until the last few days. I know now. One man has engineered every move. He killed that Crockett boy just as sure as though he'd held a gun up to his head and blazed away. That boy's father is the only man on our side who knows I'm here. If I'm caught it's going to go pretty hard with me—I've already been accused of being in your employ. But that's beside the point."

"Well, who is it?" the old man thundered. "Give him a name!"

Jim shook his head.

"Not yet, Mr. Stall. He belongs to me. Billy Sauls was my buddy."

There was nothing in the old man's manner to say that he believed what Montana was saying. In his heart he did. And it put a different complexion on things. For the better part of ten minutes he tried unsuccessfully to find out who it was that Montana suspected.

"No, I'll get him myself, Mr. Stall," Jim insisted.

"There's only two or three ways a man could run cattle out of this country. Wild Horse would be too dangerous. To the south, they'd have to go through Willow Vista and, further along, Quinn River. You'd know about it if that was the case—wouldn't you?"

"I'd know all right," he muttered pointedly.

"There's only one other way then—the back door, so to speak—Iron Point and Cisco."

"I've got that covered, if that's what you're driving at! What's your point?"

Montana permitted himself a grim smile. It was simple enough. If the Bar S had lost as heavily as the other side there was well on toward two hundred steers missing. If they hadn't been driven out to a shipping-point, they were being held somewhere between the Malheurs and the Junipers. He said as much.

"Hunh!" The old man's grunt was sceptical now. It was not easy to hide two hundred steers.

"And no easier to move them with as many men on the range as this! They'd have to hold 'em until the overbranding healed. If they can hold them a week, why can't they hold them a month? I don't believe they've ever been driven out. I aim to find them, if that's the case."

"Where are you going to look?"

"That's my problem, Mr. Stall. If I succeed, I want you to reconsider your stand in the valley."

"What? In what way?"

"In a dollar and cents way. There'll never be a profit

here for you as long as these Kentuckians hang on. And they'll stick it out. They're that kind."

"What, compromise with them?" The little veins in his cheeks were purple again. "Not a chance! Not a single chance!" he exclaimed, banging the table with his fist. "There's too many ifs in your talk, Montana, and they're all on your side!" He got up to indicate that the interview was over. "You want to grow up before you cross bows with me. I told you in Wild Horse I'd fight. That's what I'm doing, and I don't mean rustling cattle or burning people out of their homes by that. This thing is moving on to the end, and I'm perfectly satisfied to let it. Even if I had any reason to think of changing my mind I'd not obligate myself to anything on ifs. If ever you have any facts to present, I'll listen to 'em; but I'm not compromising anything."

Jim left. Old Slick-ear had more letters to write but he sat at his desk without reaching for his pen, deep in thought. He could no longer ignore Letty's continued interest in Montana. His frown deepened as he considered it.

"That's why she came here," he told himself. "That's why she had to make that long trip to Wild Horse. . . . Always defending him."

He went back to the days at Willow Vista when Jim had worked for him. He found plenty to substantiate what he was thinking.

"Began way back there," he mused. " . . . Breaking horses for her. Teaching her how to ride."

He also recalled how Montana had come to him and asked for his wages. His work had been more than satisfactory. He had not asked for more money. It had been hard to understand at the time—harder than it was now.

"No question about her having been responsible," he argued. Just how, he could not decide. "Evidently he figured he was over his head and took that way out." It gave him a new respect for Montana. "Cost me a good man," he thought, only to add, "but of course he did the right thing. He knew what I'd say about anything like that. But the nerve of him, coming here thinking I might compromise!" The very thought won a snort of contempt from him. "I've got the skids under them right now. I'll show Montana what he's up against."

He picked up his pen and reached for a sheet of paper. For once he found it difficult to begin his letter.

"Biggest mistake I ever made in my life letting that man get away from me," he muttered. "I could use him now."

CHAPTER XVIII

THUNDERING HOOFS

MONTANA was escorted to the Bar S line. It was indicative of the contempt in which he was held that the two men detailed to the task, both old acquaintances, chose to ride fifty yards to the rear.

They parted without a word, down the Big Powder, and Jim continued on alone. He was well satisfied with what he had accomplished. The old man's bluster did not disturb him.

"He wants facts, eh?" he mused. "Well, he'll get them. If Dan won't play it my way I'll dare Jubal Stark into riding with me on Quantrell's trail. I'm going to stay with him until I've got him dead to rights!"

It would have been much pleasanter to dream about Letty Stall. It was all he could do to put her out of his thoughts and confine himself to the task immediately before him.

No premonition of disaster rested on him as he rode along, and it was not until he was within several miles of the Forks that he began to move more cautiously, thinking only to avoid being seen by some chance rider from below. Therefore, he was hardly prepared to be hailed guardedly a few minutes later. It was a rude awakening. With the agility of a cat he slid out of his saddle and leaped into the willows. Getting his bearings, he looked up and saw Plenty Eagles signing to him.

"What are you doing down here?" Montana asked sharply.

"All the time I am watching Quantrell," the Piute replied stonily. "Always knowing where he goes. Thinking I have to kill him this morning."

It provoked Montana.

"Didn't I tell you to leave him to me?" he demanded.

"He see you with the girl. One of his men with him. Want to shoot you," the Indian informed him. "Afraid for you."

Jim tossed away his cigarette and gazed at him keenly for a moment.

"Your heart is good, *Cola*," he said. "Quantrell won't make me any trouble."

"Making you plenty trouble right now," Plenty Eagles insisted.

"How?"

Jim's eyes clouded as the Indian began to unfold his tale of the trap into which he had been riding.

"Not hearing what they say," the boy went on, "except you are spy. Quantrell make plenty talk. Not living long if they seeing you."

The news floored Montana for a minute. What a sorry mess he had made of things! Plans? He had no plans now. In his despair he told himself he could not have more deliberately delivered himself into Quantrell's hands had he tried. He had thought to force a showdown. Well, here was one—and he was on the wrong end of it.

"I guess this puts me on the shelf as far as this fight is concerned," he groaned. He made Plenty Eagles repeat his story of how Quantrell and Shorty had observed his meeting with Letty, and how the big fellow had then raced south for Gault and the others.

"What he had to say fell on willing ears," he thought, his mouth grim. "No use thinking I could explain. Quantrell would never wait for that. He'd stop me before I could open my mouth, and if he needed an excuse for putting a slug into me he'd claim self-defense."

He asked Plenty Eagles how far they were from the ambush.

"Mebbe one mile——"

"That's far enough for a minute," Jim muttered. "They can't have seen me yet."

"No, not seeing you from here."

Montana knew nothing was to be gained by trying to slip around them. He was through down below. They'd come to the Box C and lead him out to the nearest tree. Dan Crockett was the only man he could summon to his defense.

"If they grab me they'll never wait for Dan to talk," he thought.

At Jim's suggestion they left their horses in the bottom and climbed a hogback that gave them a view far down the creek. Montana could discover no glimpse of the men, but Plenty Eagles finally was able to point out their tethered horses.

It was answer enough. He nodded to the boy and they returned to their ponies.

"That's the finish," Jim told him, "I'm through."

"Mebbe you not through," Plenty Eagles answered cryptically.

Jim gave him a questioning glance.

"What do you mean?"

"You telling me watch Quantrell . . . I watch him."

"Yeah?" His throat was tight.

"Plenty cattle being rustled. . . . You knowing who get them?"

"*Cola!*" It was cry of relief. " . . . You know who got them, eh?"

The Indian nodded gravely. "Me—I know," he said.

Jim caught him by the shoulders.

"Quantrell and his bunch?" he demanded.

"Yes—get him all." Plenty Eagles' face was stolid, but he was enjoying himself immensely to find himself so important.

"You saw 'em cut them out?"

"Plenty time. See you yesterday on cutbank. You make talk with Quantrell. He and Shorty go. . . .Get six steer from Joe Gault before come home."

Jim's eyes were snapping with eagerness.

"Well, what he's doing with them, Plenty Eagles? Not sending them out."

"No——" He was not to be hurried. His information was too precious to be tossed out recklessly.

"Where's he got them?"

"In the mine."

"What?" It took Montana's breath away.

"In the mine," Plenty Eagles repeated. "My father not going to the creek for water like Quantrell say. Yesterday I think to myself: 'Why he lie about that?' About daylight I go to the mine. Once I work there. The upper level is cut through. Come out other side from house. I crawl in. Cattle there. Mebbe two hundred head. Soon Quantrell come. Bring more steers. Not seeing me." The Piute shook his head regretfully. "But for you I am killing him. . . . Plenty water down below. Nobody ever finding him."

Words were beyond Montana. He knew he had victory and vindication in his grasp if he could take advantage of the knowledge that was now his.

"Pretty big surprise, eh?" the boy grinned.

"Takes my breath away," Jim got out. "He was smarter than I thought. Smooth business using the old mine. I missed that play clean." His head was throbbing. "I don't know what it's going to be worth to me now. Yesterday the information would have been priceless."

"Not be sure until daylight," Plenty Eagles explained. "I stay down to find you. When I see Quantrell tracking you I think better I watch him. . . . Good thing, too."

"You said it, *Cola!* I'd be a dead mackerel right now but for you."

He did not intend to end the matter by running away. He had asked for cards. They had been dealt him. He was holding a royal flush now. He would play it some way.

He considered several moves, but dismissed them as promising too little hope of success. The minutes were fleeing. He realized that he dared not tarry there much longer. He knew his play had to be a one-man stand, aside from such assistance as he might have from the Indian.

Out of sheer desperation, he hit upon a plan that satisfied him. It was dangerous, and had to be nicely timed to be successful. But he felt he had to chance it. He outlined it to Plenty Eagles.

Its daring appealed to the Piute, but he shook his head. "Something go wrong," he said.

"What can go wrong if you do as I say?" Jim asked sharply. "We'll trade horses. I'll give you my hat. They won't grow suspicious until you're near enough to be recognized. By that time I will have cut across the hills and be almost as far as Quantrell's house. Quantrell's bunch will see me. The men across the creek won't. Too many trees. There can't be anything wrong with that."

"Then what I do?"

"You stay on the east bank so you'll run into Gault. As soon as Quantrell sees me heading for the mine he'll know what's up. They'll try to stop me. And they'll pull away from the creek without letting the rest know. When Gault questions you, give him this message: tell him the cattle are in the mine—to come quick! You savvy all that?"

Plenty Eagles nodded weightily.

"That's all you've got to do. I'll take care of the rest."

Plenty Eagles' horse was a tough, wiry cayuse with a mean eye. He could travel, though. Montana soon was moving away from the creek, keeping to an arroyo that concealed him effectively. Three hundred yards from the house he was forced out in the open. He had no way of knowing whether anyone was there or not. He could only hope that Quantrell had drawn all of his men to the creek.

"I'll find out in a hurry," he ground out as he flashed by the house.

Nothing happened. He could look back and see the Big Powder now.

"They haven't spotted me yet," he told himself. "I'll go through with this whether they do or not." Without looking back, he raked his horse with his spurs and drove on toward the old Adelaide. When he flung himself out of the saddle at the fence and flashed another glance toward the Big Powder, a cry of satisfaction broke from him. Seven men were streaking away from the creek and racing toward him!

"They can't get here for ten minutes—and that's time enough!" he thought.

Ten yards inside of the mouth of the mine he found another gate. He shot the lock off. His nose told him, even before his eyes, that the steers were there.

It was dark in the tunnels. It took him a moment to get the lay of things. The cattle were on the upper level. They objected to his presence and began to bawl. Talking to them, Montana edged through.

It took him precious minutes to reach the drift that came out on the opposite side of the mountain.

"There's wind enough through here to do the trick," he muttered. The shoring and beams were dry with age. "They'll burn, all right!"

It was only a few seconds before the tiny blaze he kindled was licking up the timbers. The wind was carrying the smudge toward the mine entrance. Already the cattle were moving away from him, bawling loudly. Their cries echoed weirdly in his ears.

"Another minute is all I want!" he assured himself.

He was playing it fine. Already Quantrell and his men were coming up the side cañon. A wisp of smoke was curling out of the mouth of the mine.

"He's firin' it!" Quantrell shouted as he leaped the fence. He was past wondering whether it was Montana. It couldn't be anyone else. "We got to get in there in a hurry!"

The others followed him over the fence. Shorty paused to glance back at the valley.

"Here the rest come!" he yelled. "The jig's up fer sure!"

Quantrell stopped in his tracks. A groan of dismay broke from him. He began to curse. The wrath of the men he had duped could never be stayed now.

"Why didn't I let you git him this morning, Shorty?" he raged. "God a'mighty, we ain't got a chance! We're penned up like rats in a trap!" He began to curse incoherently.

"Aw, shut up!" Shorty screamed at him. "Your chatter won't git you nothin'!"

"You said it!" another growled. "I always thought you'd fold up if it got hot. What are we goin' to do?"

"I'm fannin' it!" Shorty cried. "You can stick it out here if you want to. Not me!"

"You fool!" Quantrell screamed at him. "We're better off here behind the planks than out there in the open! We can shoot this out and get away!"

"By God, we'll have to shoot it out! It's too late to go now! You made it sweet fer us!"

The fire was forgotten in the face of their new danger. Gault seemed to be in charge. He deployed his men up the sides of the cañon.

"Pick 'em off!" Quantrell yelled. "Don't let 'em get above us!"

Guns began to bark. Both sides were firing. A slug got Shorty through the shoulder. He retrieved his rifle, and propping it into position, began to blaze away with his left hand. All of them knew they were fighting for their lives. The best they could hope for was a slug or a rope.

Quantrell began to fall apart. Shorty cursed him. In their extremity, he was the real leader.

Unnoticed by them, the volume of smoke pouring out of the mine had doubled and redoubled. Suddenly the cries of the maddened steers reached them.

Quantrell understood if the others didn't.

It chilled the marrow in his bones. A bullet spattered against the wall beside him. It went unnoticed as he stared with mouth open at the black maw of the mine. All of his bullying was gone. He knew they didn't have a chance. Hugging the walls, the plank fence barring the way, they were indeed like rats in a trap! When that maddened avalanche of thundering hoofs and goring horns poured out of the mine it would grind them into the dust.

Crazed as he was with fear, he knew his only hope of escape lay within the mine. If he could reach it before the inner gate went down, he might hope to find safety in one of the cross tunnels.

He did not tarry. Unmindful of the guns above, he ran for the entrance. It was only a yard away when he heard the inner gate crash. It went down with a ripping, splintering sound that turned his blood to ice. With eyes starting from their sockets he plunged into the smoke.

He was not out of the way a second too soon. With a deafening bellow the crazed cattle swept by him, heads lowered and horns flashing.

Here was death—relentless, inexorable! A strangled scream broke from the trapped men. Horses reared and dashed away, eyes rolling with fear.

Shorty threw away his gun and leaped for the fence. The others were only a step behind him. Gault and his neighbors, who had only within the hour come to realize that Quantrell was their real enemy, held their fire as they looked on, white of face.

With a sickening thud the fence went down, ripped to kindling. Nothing could stop that maddened rush. The steers swept out into the valley and the dust settled down on the battered, lifeless forms they left in their wake.

Gault and Stark and the other valley men stood petrified. The poor, lifeless wretches before them did not excite them to pity. They were thinking of Montana. It slowly dawned on them that they had played a despicable rôle. Despite their scourging and doubting of him Jim had remained faithful to their cause. In their hearts they knew they must stand ashamed before the world until they had squared themselves with him.

"I feel like crawlin' into a hole and draggin' my tail in after me," Jubal said. "I been a fool and a skunk! Montana was right from the first. I can see it now. Quantrell burned me out. He raised all this hell so he could rustle our cattle. If we'd had a drop of real faith in Jim Montana most of this misery could have been avoided."

"I'll say amen to that," Gault muttered. "He did for us what we didn't have the brains nor courage to do ourselves. He's in there somewhere, burnin' to death, and I'm goin' in ter get him! Don't ferget Quantrell's in there, too!"

"I'll go with you!" Jubal exclaimed. "I'm prayin' to God we'll find Montana. As fer that coyote Quantrell—I'm a sayin': Let him stay there. It'll save us spoilin' a good rope on him!"

CHAPTER XIX

THE END OF HIS TETHER

PLENTY EAGLES had ridden to the mine with the valley men. The dust had not yet settled behind the stampeding steers when he slid down the wall and rushed for the entrance. Gault called to him, but the young Indian did not stop.

In a few moments all were at the mouth of the tunnel. Even there the smoke was bad.

"Don't believe we can git in," young Lance declared doubtfully.

"No? If thet young buck's got guts enough to risk her, I hev!" Jubal exclaimed. "I'm agoin' in!"

Before he had taken a step Plenty Eagles staggered out, coughing violently. His eyebrows and hair were badly singed.

"Too much smoke," he gasped. "Not getting in there——"

Jubal insisted on trying to get in. It was only a minute or two he tottered out, lungs bursting. It was a few seconds before he was able to speak.

"Both on 'em is trapped in there," he said, still trying to catch his breath.

"My God, do we have to stand here unable to do anythin'?" Gault exclaimed miserably. "Ain't there somethin' we can do? Didn't they drive one of the tunnels through on t'other side of the mountain?"

"Yeh, I knowing the place!" Plenty Eagles spoke up. "I show you where!"

He ran to his horse and leaped into the saddle. Fanning the pony with his quirt, he was away before the others had even started.

The animal floundered in the loose rock, sending tons of it rolling down hill. The Piute kept his horse on its feet, however, and raced on, to bring the pony to a slithering stop when he reached the tunnel.

There was very little smoke there now. Encouraged, he rushed in.

He had not gone over twenty yards when a groan of despair was wrung from him. The ceiling of the old tunnel had caved in. . . . Tons of rocks sealed the passage.

Gault and Jubal found him trying to worm his way through.

"You'll have the rest of it down on us if you keep that up," Gault warned. "We couldn't clean enough of that rock away to git through in a week."

"No other chance," Plenty Eagles ground out as he continued to tug at the huge blocks of quartz. His fingers were bleeding. Suddenly a booming sound warned him that Gault had been right. They ran back in time to escape being crushed.

"No chance now," the young Indian muttered stonily.

There was nothing for them to do but go back to the mouth of the mine and wait, hoping against hope, that some miracle might save Montana.

When the tunnel that they had found blocked had first caved in, Jim was only a short distance away. A beam had burned through. As it snapped in two a deafening roar warned him in time and he leaped clear.

With that avenue of escape blocked, he tried to rush out through the main tunnel. The heat and smoke were terrific. Bursting lungs soon convinced him that he could never make it. Hands and face burned, he crawled back toward the cave-in, knowing he must soon suffocate unless he found a cross-cut or managed to get on another level.

With a burning brand for a torch, he found a drift that took him out of the main tunnel. The air was better. His shirt was burning. He yanked it off. His back was a torture. Every nerve seemed to be in agony. He knew he had to go on. The fire would work in there before long.

In a few moments his improvised torch flickered out, leaving him in inky darkness. He had to feel every inch of the way, afraid lest he plunge headlong into one of the deep shafts.

The drift seemed to be pitching downward. He

wondered if it was only a ramp leading to the flooded lower level. He had cut himself off completely if that were so.

He had lost all sense of direction. At times he thought he was moving toward the mouth of the mine, and then again, that he was circling away from it. Once his hand touched water. His heart sank. But it was only a spring, seeping down the side of the tunnel. He found a pool where the water had gathered, and he bathed his blistered face and hands.

As he waited there, a distant muffled booming told him there had been another cave-in. He estimated that he had been in the mine almost an hour. His matches were exhausted; his watch was of no use. With a sickening dread, he realized that a man could wander about in those old workings for days without ever finding a way out.

Certainly Gault and Stark must have come to their senses by now. They would make some effort to find him.

"If they don't, Plenty Eagles will," he thought. It gave him courage.

The drift was not pitching downward any longer. Moving forward on hands and knees, his progress was slow. Without warning he put out a hand and could not find the floor of the drift. He drew back hurriedly and began to explore with his fingers. A shaft yawned in front of him. He picked up a rock and dropped it into the hole. He heard it splash far below.

It was possible that the drift ended there, but it was more likely that two or three tunnels came into the shaft, radiating in several directions. He found the latter surmise correct as he got around the shaft safely. It was a question which tunnel he should take.

"I'll go straight ahead," he decided. "I can find my way back here if I have to."

As he rested there he heard a man cough. It was a startling interruption. He was about to call out when a light appeared in the tunnel he was following. A man was holding a torch aloft. The man was Quantrell! Montana's cry froze on his lips before he could utter it.

Quantrell walked unsteadily. He was naked from the waist up, his body scorched and blackened. Jim could only surmise how he came to be there. The big fellow did not glance back over his shoulder as he would have done if he feared pursuit. No trace of his surly defiance remained.

"He's trapped with me," Jim thought. "That's rich —the two of us alone down here together!" Montana got to his feet noiselessly. Quantrell was sure to see him in another second.

"That's far enough!" he called out.

It stopped the big fellow in his tracks. His body stiffened as he balanced on his toes, his eyes narrowing with hatred as surprise passed. With a cry of rage as fierce as the snarl of a grizzly, he hurled his torch at Montana.

It fell harmlessly to the floor of the tunnel, casting

weird shadows over them as it burned fitfully. Quantrell slapped his hand to his holster. He sucked in his breath sharply, his eyes bulging horribly. His gun was not there!

Montana caught the movement of his hand.

"Go ahead—and I'll bust you where you stand!" he warned. "My finger's itching to let you have it!"

Quantrell's arm dropped limply to his side. "You get pretty damn gabby when you got the heel of a six-gun in your fist and the other fellow ain't got nothin' in the leather!" he snarled. "Put your gun away and I'll make you eat what I've had on the fire so long for you!"

"That's okay with me!" Montana flung back at him. He jammed his gun into the holster. "And there won't be any running out this time," he advised. "You're going to stand up and take it. You've been handing it out to me for a long time—and its backing up on you right now!"

In weight and size the advantage was all with Quantrell. The narrow tunnel was to his liking, too. He ached to get his long arms around Montana and throttle the life out him. With an animal-like grunt, he lowered his head and charged.

Jim stepped aside and gave him a stinging blow that straightened him up. Once more the big fellow cursed and came at him, and again Montana drove his fist into his face. He had put everything he had into the blow, and it amazed him to see Quantrell weather it. He knew he couldn't hit harder.

They fought on, Quantrell lowering his head and rushing him repeatedly, trying to drag him into his embrace. Hit and get away—that was Montana's chance.

In the course of fifteen minutes he had cut Quantrell's face to ribbons, but the big fellow came on for more. Jim was tiring. He had to hurt him soon— stop those mad rushes. All his long-stored-up hatred of the man was unleashed.

Suddenly Quantrell brought his long right up. It caught Jim as he was backing away, but it split his lip. He could taste the blood as it trickled into his mouth.

Quantrell seemed to sense that Jim was tiring. He wasn't getting away so fast any more. He managed to clip him again. A hoarse, insensate cry rumbled up out of his throat.

"Go on, slash away!" he thought. "I'll hammer the brains out of you before we're through. But for your damned meddlin' I'd never got in this fix!"

His makeshift torch began to sputter out. He turned to kick it out of the way and Montana caught him off balance. The blow drove his head against the wall with a thud that made his senses reel.

The torch was only a glowing ember now. Quantrell could just make out Montana's hunched figure. He threw caution to the winds and charged him like an infuriated bull.

Jim threw himself flat to avoid him. Quantrell grabbed at him frantically and missed as he tried to stay his mad rush. He had seen the yawning shaft. With flailing arms he tried to stop himself. His foot went out and found nothing under it. With a strangled scream of fear he tried to whirl, even then, to save himself.

He was falling . . . His fingers slipped over the edge——

Montana sat up and stared after him unseeingly. Heart standing still, he listened. Seconds passed before he heard the body strike the water below.

He picked up the red coal that had been the torch and tried to blow it into flame. Holding it before him, he peered down into the depths of the shaft.

"Quantrell!" he shouted. "Quantrell!"

There was no answer. Weak and exhausted, Montana crept back from the brink, his breath coming in gasps. It was good just to stretch out on the cold rocky floor and not think.

He never wanted to move again. He told himself the smoke was not any heavier than it had been. Maybe the fire in the main tunnel was burning out. Later on he'd try to retrace the way Quantrell had come. Maybe it would lead him out. Maybe he'd end up down some shaft, too. He was almost too weary to care.

He was still lying there when Plenty Eagles and the others found him, early that evening.

CHAPTER XX

THE FOREMAN OF SQUAW VALLEY

WITHOUT agreement of any sort, both sides seemed to have declared a truce. The steers Quantrell had rustled had been rounded up and the Bar S yearlings cut out. Old Slick-ear's men had been told to come down and get their stuff. They drove it off unmolested.

Montana had been carried to the Box C. Mother Crockett reported that he was resting easy. News of what he had done travelled north with Reb. Letty Stall got the story from him five minutes after he had reported to her father. It filled her with an anxiety she did not try to conceal.

"Reb—tell me the truth, is he dangerously injured?"

"Reckon not. Guess he's sufferin' plenty; but nothin' serious about it."

She saw that Reb was none too happy over having to sing Jim's praises.

"Did you see him?" she asked.

"No. Reckon he ain't hankerin' to see any of us."

Letty said no more, but she was determined to see Jim at once, and with that thought in mind, she marched into her father's presence.

Old Slick-ear's brow was creased in a puzzled frown. He was not surprised to see his daughter. He knew she would get the facts from Reb, and because he suspected her interest in Montana, lose no time in confronting him.

Now that she had come, he waited for her to speak. He was singularly ill at ease. The turn events had taken confounded him.

"Well, Father, you told Jim you wanted facts," Letty declared. "You'll have to admit you have them."

"So it would seem," he admitted gruffly.

"I want to know what you are going to do?"

"Do? What do you expect me to do?" he demanded, bristling as usual. "Do you think I'm going to crawl to those people just because Montana has proved me wrong about one or two things? Not on your life! If the violence is over, I'm glad. But that doesn't end the matter."

Letty pretended a great surprise.

"I wasn't intimating that it did," she corrected him. "I've often heard you say you were in the cattle business to make money. You know by now you'll never make a profit here unless some compromise is effected. Those people can't lose with men like Jim to lead them."

"No—?" He could have changed her mind about that. If he didn't, it was due principally to the fact—which he never would have admitted—that he no longer knew his own mind. "What's your idea?" he grunted sceptically.

"Well, I think you might talk things over with them. Jim did something for you as well as for his own people in rounding up Quantrell's gang. The decent thing for you to do would be to go and see him. I know I intend to go. If we can do anything for him, we should."

"Hunh?" He loved her spunk. "Well, I'll think it over pretty carefully," he announced.

"And while you're thinking it over, I'll be riding down there!" she informed him very positively. She started to leave the room.

"Wait a minute, Letty!" he exclaimed, his manner as severe as ever. "I want to talk to you——"

"Well——"

He tried to transfix her with his eyes.

"Are you in love with Jim Montana?"

It was breath-taking. But she was his daughter, and she answered him with equal directness.

"I am," she said. She drew herself up to await his outburst.

"Hunh! *Hunh!*" Old Slick-ear pushed his chair away and began walking the floor. "Does he know it?" he shot out.

"Hardly," Letty smiled. Her self-possession surprised her. "I'm waiting for you to tell me he is only a fifty-dollar-a-month cowpuncher and that I'm seven kinds of a fool."

"See here!" he thundered, fixing his fierce old eyes on her again. "Let me do my own talking! Montana's no fool; I always said he was a good man. He doesn't have to be a fifty-dollar-a-month hand if he doesn't want to. He'd never have left me but for you."

It was Letty's turn to be surprised.

"Better tell me what you're thinking," she advised icily.

"Good Lord, you don't think for a minute I didn't know about this, do you?" he demanded furiously. "I've got eyes and some sense. When a good-looking cowpuncher begins breaking horses and pointing out beautiful scenery to the boss' daughter a man can draw his own conclusions. He tried to get away from you but you wouldn't take no for an answer."

"You knew all this time—and said nothin'?" Letty was frankly incredulous. "Father, tell me—are you really so angry or are you just teasing me?"

"I don't know what I am," he grumbled. "I ought to be angry. I don't suppose Jim Montana's got a hundred dollars to his name. On the other hand, I've been afraid all along that you'd fall in love with one of those white-collar dudes I've been stumbling over every time I came home for the last three years. I've got you everything else you wanted, haven't I? If you've got your heart set on Montana, I guess I'll have to get him for you, too."

Letty threw her arms around him and kissed him affectionately. "You're a precious old bear," she trilled.

"But don't you try to 'get him' for me—as you put it. I'm too afraid I might lose him."

"Lose him?" he snorted. "Hunh! Didn't I tell you the man is no fool? But don't fool yourself that I'm going to let up on him."

"He hasn't asked you to—" Letty reminded him.

That afternoon they set out for the Box C. News of their coming ran ahead of them. When they arrived, they found old Lance and Dave Morrow talking to Crockett. Their attitude was one of watchful waiting rather than hostility.

"Can we see him?" Mr. Stall asked.

"Reckon you can," Dan answered. "Jest step inside."

Despite his protests, Jim now occupied the front room.

Mother Crockett met them in the kitchen and showed them in to him. Jim's face was swathed in bandages. He had dozed off for the moment. Letty fell to her knees beside him, her eyes misty. Unmindful of her father's presence, she lowered her head and brushed Jim's lips with her own.

It awakened Montana. For long seconds he stared up at her incredulously. "Am I dreaming?" he murmured.

For answer, she kissed him again.

"It was wonderful, Jim," she smiled. "I'm so proud of you! I suppose you are suffering terribly."

"It's not so bad now," he smiled. "I'll be all right directly."

The old man cleared his throat by way of making his presence known. Jim blushed like a schoolboy. "Guess there's no need of my saying anything, Mr. Stall."

The old man pulled his brows down. "I don't know what you could say," he declared, a twinkle in his eyes. "Looks to me as though you're hooked."

His manner changed abruptly when their conversation turned to talk of a compromise. They discussed the matter for nearly an hour.

"I'll not move out of this valley," old Slick-ear insisted doggedly. "You know me, Montana; when I get my brand on a steer it stays there; when I buy an acre of land I buy it! There's one thing I will do. This Quantrell property will come up for sale. I want the right to buy it in without opposition. I want Dave Morrow to sell me about a quarter section above the North Fork. Crockett will have to sell me about the same amount. That'll give me an unbroken piece of range. With that, and by cutting a slice off of Willow Vista I'd have a going concern here." He had not come there to say anything of the sort. It surprised him more than Letty. "If they'll agree to that I'll consent to forming a water district here so we'll all have as much as we need. And of course I'll need a foreman to make it show a profit. I expect you could do it."

Montana found himself as inarticulate as Plenty Eagles.

"The foreman of Squaw Valley!" Letty beamed.

Doesn't that thrill you, Jim? You've got to make them see it!"

"Well, they've got the land and you've got the water," Montana smiled. "I don't see how they can say no."

"You can put it up to them right now if you want to," the old man volunteered. "They're outside."

"All right, call them in!"

Crockett and the Morrows listened respectfully as Jim outlined the plan. When he had finished, they withdrew to the far end of the room and conferred in whispers. It did not take them long to reach a decision. Dan acted as spokesman for them.

"We agree to it," he said simply. "A man never had a better friend than Montana's been to us. I been hit harder than most; I lost my boy. But I reckon the thing to do is shake hands and forgit all the misunderstandin' and be neighbors."

"We'll do it that way then," old Slick-ear agreed. "I'll write my attorneys to-night. It will take a week for one of them to get here. You'll want a lawyer to represent you. Say we get together a week from to-day at my ranch. Montana will be able to ride by that time."

That arrangement was satisfactory to all. Mr. Stall shook hands with them and followed them out of the room. Letty lingered behind for a moment.

"I can't believe it, Letty," Jim murmured reverently as he gazed at her. "I've just been pinching myself to see if I were really awake. I guess there hasn't been a day since I first met you that I haven't dreamed of making you my wife. Of late it's been a nightmare; it seemed so hopeless." Self-consciousness forced his eyes down. ". . . I always loved you, Letty."

"Don't you suppose I knew?" she whispered, tremulously.

"I guess you did at that——"

"I had all I could do to keep from throwing my arms about you and saying, 'Here I am; take me,' when we met on the creek."

Jim shook his head. "I still can't believe it," he said. "I'm sure the fire and smoke must have affected my mind. To see you here and have you say you love me is incredible enough, but your father—his offer to compromise—his attitude toward me——"

"It's true enough, Jim," Letty smiled, "but don't be taken in by Father's attitude. He'll do all he can to make it as difficult for us as possible until he's utterly unbearable. Then he'll do one of his amazing right-about-faces and be the most tractable person in the world."

Letty suggested that it might be wise to take Jim into Wild Horse.

"I couldn't have better treatment than I'm getting here," he declared. "Mother Crockett is quite a doctor herself. I guess everybody in the valley has been here asking after me."

Letty said she would be down again before the week was over.

"I'd sure like to see you," he said, "but I don't think it would be wise for you to come. It's going to take these people a few days to adjust themselves to the new order of things. It'll be better if they're left to themselves for awhile."

Letty saw the wisdom of such a course.

"It will be a week then before I see you," she sighed. "It will seem ages."

Montana found himself agreeing with her as the days passed. He wanted to be up and about again. Mother Crockett finally consented. When the bandages were removed Jim found his face had healed nicely. He had scars on his arms that he would carry for life.

Unfortunately, the peace that had settled over the valley could not bring back happiness to the Box C. The Crocketts could not help thinking of Gene and how needlessly he had been sacrificed.

Four days after Letty and her father had been there, Montana saddled Paint and took his first ride since the fire. It was pleasant in the hills. His heart was singing with happiness. His future was bright with promise.

Toward evening he turned his horse toward home, cutting through the reservation. He had reached the crest of the last saddle when he saw a rider moving rapidly up the Skull. The pace at which he rode hinted that he came on urgent business. Montana could not make out who it was. A vague feeling of disaster touched him, and he turned Paint so that he could intercept the stranger.

The man was none other than Graham Rand.

Jim felt his throat tighten. This could not herald good news. Graham would not have punished his horse to come with tidings of victory.

Rand did not waste any time on a greeting.

"Jim, it's happened; the sale of the reservation has been held unlawful! I got the news out of Vickers this morning. The whole matter is going to be thrown into the courts."

It was a blow that left Montana speechless for moments. With victory in his grasp—the quarrel settled—this had to come up!

News of the compromise in the valley had drifted into Wild Horse. Rand could appreciate what his message meant to Montana.

"If it only had come a week later," Jim groaned. "You know Mr. Stall will never go through with it now. When these valley men get the news it's going to stagger them. They'll end up by blaming me. I led them to hope again—and it is going to be like knocking a cup of water out of the hands of a man dying with thirst to make them face this."

"Well, I figure you've got a day or two of grace," Rand said. "The old man can't know yet."

"No, Graham! You're suggesting something that you wouldn't do yourself. As badly as I feel about this I wouldn't try to jam the deal through. Mr. Stall offered to play fair—and I've got to play that way, too. What do you suppose he'd think of me if I tricked him into this? He'd have a legal out. He'd use it. I'd be through and this crowd down here would be worse off than ever."

"I suspected you'd feel that way," Rand replied. "On the way over I've been trying to figure every out you had."

"The only out for me is to see the old man at once and put my cards on the table. I don't know what I'll be able to say . . . It's just about hopeless, Graham."

"It's tough to go through what you did and have it come to nothing," Rand murmured thoughtfully. "You've got to play the string out now, Jim, and if the game goes against you, keep your head up."

They talked it over thoroughly.

"Better come up to the house," Jim suggested. "You'll have to stay here over night."

"Think not," said Rand. "They'd wonder why I was here. Time enough for them to know about this after you've seen the old man. I'll go back to Furnace Creek and stay there to-night."

In the morning, in order to get away without exciting Dan's curiosity, Montana said he was going up to have a look at the mine. Brent offered to go with him.

"No, I'll have to take it easy," Jim countered. "I may not get back until evening."

Once out of sight of the ranch he showed no sign of taking it easy. He forced his pony where the going was good. By eleven o'clock he was in sight of the Bar S house. Down by the corrals the men were putting the roof on the new bunk-house.

Jim was glad to escape them for the moment. He could see nothing of Letty or her father. The door stood open, however, and he walked in. Old Slick-ear was at his desk, writing as usual.

"Good-morning, Mr. Stall," Montana said by way of announcing his presence. Old Slick-ear gave him a fierce glance.

"Well, what brings you here?" he demanded brusquely. "You don't look none too happy."

"I've come to throw myself on your mercy, Mr. Stall."

"Hunh?" The old man's mouth straightened. "I thought we'd settled all that. You backing out now?"

"No, it's not that," said Jim. "I reckon it's a case of giving you a chance to back out. I'd do anything I could to see the arrangement we made carried through. But we couldn't get anywhere unless we were shooting square on both sides. Something has come up that compels me to tell you that we can't hold you to your bargain."

"Yes?" he glared. "What is it?"

Jim hesitated over his answer. "I'll never move him," he thought. "Well," he said finally, "you warned me in Wild Horse that I was over my head; that you would have the sale thrown out by the Land Office . . . I got word last evening that you'd won."

Their voices had drawn Letty from her room. She

came down the stairs hurriedly to find the two men confronting each other, her father's manner as fierce as Jim's face was glum.

"Jim—why are you here? Is something wrong?"

"Something's decidedly right!" her father exclaimed.

"Evidently—by the way you're gloating," said Letty.

"The Land Office has thrown out the Squaw Valley sale," old Slick-ear informed her. "I've got good reason to crow!"

"So that's what brought Seth MacMasters here! You've known for days that the sale had been declared void."

"Why—" Montana was having trouble understanding. Mr. Stall had taken his news as though it were a real surprise. Letty came to his rescue.

"Don't be distressed, Jim," she said. "Father knew long before we came to see you that the decision was in his favor. I suppose he has been threatening to back out on the agreement."

"Is that right, Mr. Stall?" Montana demanded, his jaws clenched.

The old man took another turn about the room and then came back to his desk. "Sit down, Jim—and you, too, Letty," he said. "I'll do a little talking now. Of course I knew the decision was in my favor. I even arranged for Vickers to let the information slip out to Rand and one or two others, figuring they'd get it to you. Now I'll tell you why.

"When I made that offer down at Crockett's place

there was a reservation in the back of my mind. You two are in love with each other. You're going to be my son-in-law, Jim. I said to myself, 'I'll test him. If he tries to jam this deal through, thinking he's taking advantage of me, he'll never marry my daughter. If he shoots square—I'm with him all the way.' "

A long-drawn sigh of relief escaped Montana. A smile came back to his lips. "Then the deal stands?"

"That's what I said," Mr. Stall grumbled. "It's costing me plenty. If Letty had kept out of this a few minutes longer I'd have got some sort of a dividend out of you." The dinner bell broke in on him. "Better come in and sit down with us," he invited.

Jim could only shake his head. He felt a little dizzy.

"He's a hard man to have riding herd on you," he said to Letty.

"Yes—and his daughter takes after him," she smiled back.